THE GIRL
WITH THE
CRAZY BROTHER

THE GIRL WITH THE CRAZY BROTHER

A Novel by Betty Hyland

A Modern Version

Copyright © 2002 by Betty Hyland.

ISBN :   Softcover   1-4010-7448-0

All rights reserved. No part of this book may be reproduced or transmitted in any form or by any means, electronic or mechanical, including photocopying, recording, or by any information storage and retrieval system, without permission in writing from the copyright owner.

This is a work of fiction. Names, characters, places and incidents either are the product of the author's imagination or are used fictitiously, and any resemblance to any actual persons, living or dead, events, or locales is entirely coincidental.

This book was printed in the United States of America.

To order additional copies of this book, contact:
Xlibris Corporation
1-888-795-4274
www.Xlibris.com
Orders@Xlibris.com
16461

in memory of Mark

CHAPTER ONE

Dana McAllister stood by the lockers in the modern glass and formica hallway of Wilson High School, in Pasadena, California, a thin girl with straight brown hair and hazel eyes. She stared at key number 696, which had been issued to her in homeroom this first day of her junior year. She wished she were back in Paul Revere High, her old two-story brick school in Boston, Massachusetts, where all her friends were.

The key didn't fit the lock.

Kids stampeded down the hall, dropping books, slamming locker doors, shouting to one another, while Dana told herself, don't panic. It's just a key.

She took a deep breath and glanced at the kids around her. They'd probably known each other forever, maybe even since kindergarten, just like she knew her old friends back home. Why did her father's engineering company have to transfer him to California? She'd *hated* the idea, pleaded with her parents to let her live with Aunt Deb, at least until she was out of high school.

You could practically *walk* to the school from Aunt Deb's, but it didn't do any good. They made her move.

Her father kept saying, "You'll meet new friends, Dana. This is an opportunity for the whole family."

Her mother had only said, "Go for it, Clark. I can set up my computer anywhere. Readers don't know where I write my stories from." She had practically started packing right away.

And her brother, Bill, had said, "I guess so, Dad." A dark look crossed Dana's face as she thought about Bill. She hoped he was doing okay over in the annex where the seniors were stuck until construction was completed on the new wing. Since they'd moved two weeks ago, he'd spent most of his time on his bed, staring at nothing. She thought about him. Well, maybe he did that in Boston, too.

"Problems?"

Dana whirled around and stared into the broad, homely/handsome grinning face of a kid with brown hair curling around his ears as he bent to examine the key. "I'm Ian Quinn, your friendly locker checker." He looked at her with frank brown eyes.

"It doesn't fit." Her voice squeaked. She cleared her throat. She'd hardly spoken since leaving the house that morning.

"You're reading it upside down. It's for locker number 969. You see, the school has these surprise tests to see if you're getting as confused as you're supposed to." He winked and pointed to a locker at the end of the row.

"Thanks," she said, and hoped her ears weren't poking out of her hair. When she found the locker, she glanced back in time to see Ian Quinn stroll off with a leather camera bag slung over his shoulder. Maybe he's on the school paper, she thought. Nice kid, she decided, watching him move casually through the crowd.

Locker number 969 opened easily.

Dana's morning classes went quickly. In American Lit the *Moby Dick* books hadn't come in, so Mr. Zepeda gave everyone a handout to read. Mrs. Pelotte, the World History teacher, reminded Dana of a math teacher back in Boston who had once noted that "Dana McAllister is a nice girl to have in class." Only this teacher took a long time getting the right spelling of everyone's name and stressed the importance of "getting acquainted."

Still, Dana felt self-conscious this first day, and when noon came she wished she lived close enough to walk home for lunch. She didn't want to sit by herself and chew a whole tuna fish sandwich but she didn't want to sit just anywhere either, not knowing anybody . . . not the first day in a new school.

She held the tray steady as she surveyed the lunchroom and decided to sit at an empty table close to a back door that led out into the hall, and kind of look around.

As she unwrapped her sandwich, her mind drifted to Bill again. What was going on with him anyway? Like this morning when he wouldn't walk his cocker spaniel, Trixie, because some man on the radio told him not to go outside. Her mother had thought he meant the weatherman, and her father had talked absently about storms up north. But Dana had thought Bill needed rescuing so she walked Trixie herself. He would have done it for her. A grateful Bill had nodded thanks and darted out of the kitchen.

She snapped open her soda can.

"New?" Ian Quinn's question jolted Dana back to reality. She jumped as he placed his camera case on the lunch table, sat across from her, and began squeezing packets of catsup, relish, mustard and mayonnaise all over a hamburger.

She nodded. "We only moved to California two weeks ago. I'm really from Boston."

"From Basston, are you?" Ian said, imitating her accent.

What a nice smile he's got, Dana thought.

Silence while they chewed. Why is it so hard the first time you talk to somebody? she wondered. She took a sip of soda and vowed to make a list of topics to talk about for all occasions so she wouldn't always sound as though her brains had fallen out. She couldn't even think of anything clever to say about Boston.

Ian finished his hamburger in about five bites, drank down a chocolate milk, and began studying her face from different angles. "I'll take your picture for the school paper. What's your name?"

"Dana McAllister."

He wrote it down and began unpacking his camera.

"Short caption," he said. "New kid in town. Talks funny. Ears poke out of her hair."

"Oh, no," screamed Dana, covering her ears.

Click. The shutter snapped.

Her mouth flew open in surprise.

Click.

"Those pictures will be *awful*," she wailed, trying to make her straight hair do something beside hang down straight.

"We'll see," said Ian, unscrewing lenses and carefully repacking his camera in its case.

"Steven Spielberg Quinn at it again," said a voice behind her.

Dana turned in her seat to look up at two gorgeous people. They looked like all the pictures of California surfers she had ever seen . . . tanned, blond.

Ian pointed and said, "Eric Bergman and Joannie Fargo. This is Dana . . . what did you say?"

"McAllister."

What an amazing smile, Dana thought, continuing to stare at Eric Bergman's beautiful white teeth. He nodded to her, then turned to kids sitting down at the other end of the table. Dana looked away, embarrassed at having stared.

Joannie Fargo sat next to Ian and said, "I thought my picture was supposed to be in the first issue of the paper." She wore tight black pants, a tight, sleeveless peach colored shirt, designer boots, and a narrow, silver necklace. She had long blond hair and enormous green eyes. She's probably the most popular girl in the school, thought Dana, feeling self-conscious in her white T-shirt and jeans, wondering if her power bracelets were okay. She'd seen some other kids wearing them.

"The editor scrapped it for the feature on summer fires. I really got some good shots . . . or bad, I guess, since the fires burned so long." Ian's big square hand clutched his camera.

Joannie looked very disappointed. "Let me know if you want more pictures so I can be prepared. Better not catch *me* the way you just caught Dana here." Then, Joannie pointed toward a heavy girl with a spaghetti-stained T-shirt coming toward them with a bowl of french fries and a copy of Emily Dickinson's poems. "At least Sheila doesn't care." And then, to no one in particular she added, "How can she stand to be so messy?"

Sheila Montgomery slumped down at the table and told Dana, "Don't pay any attention to me. I have library duty every lunchtime so I sit here because it's close to the door."

Joannie pointed to the book. "Don't you ever leave time for fun?"

"Emily Dickinson is fun," replied Sheila, messing her short auburn hair with greasy fingers.

"Sheila's *career-oriented*," Eric explained. "She's the only kid I know who goes to summer school for 'enrichment'." He smiled his amazing smile at Dana, and her legs felt like strawberry yogurt. "My idea of fun is wind surfing or tennis," he added. "What about you?"

She really wanted to say she liked reading, too, but instead said, "Well, in Massachusetts" . . . she stopped herself from saying "Boston," . . . glancing at Ian, who winked . . . "I liked the winter sports, like ice skating and cross-country skiing."

"Good choice," said Eric, absently. He stood and shouted to a kid across the room. "I've put a four o'clock hold on the north tennis courts."

"I want to be happy no matter *what* I'm doing," Joannie chirped, tossing her long blond hair. "Otherwise, don't ask me."

Sheila finished the last of her fries, licked her fingers, and ran off with a wave to Dana.

Dana took another bite of her sandwich and looked around. I made a pretty good choice of table, she thought, and some of the kids at the other end looked like juniors, too.

When Dana hopped off the school bus that afternoon she stood for a minute on Lemon Grove Road admiring her new Spanish style, California home. It's kind of a nice house, she thought. Her eyes went to the red tile roof, the large wooden front door, the bougainvillea climbing to the small balcony outside her second-story bedroom. Maybe someday I'll have some kids over. She immediately thought of Eric Bergman and the others she'd met that day . . . Ian, Joannie, and Sheila. It wasn't too bad a day after all, she thought, crossing the road to her house.

A warm feeling came over Dana when she walked in the back door. Even as a little girl, she'd always loved going home. She found her mother working on her computer in a corner of the kitchen where she had set up her "office." She was a freelance writer who sold travel pieces and short stories to various newspapers and magazines. Libby McAllister, looking plump and comfy to hug, clicked the cursor on SAVE and kissed Dana on the forehead. "How was your first day?"

"It was really okay, I think." As Dana broke open a granola bar, she thought her mother looked worried about something. "Is everything okay?"

"I guess so."

Then Dana noticed her father's car in the driveway. "Where's Dad?" she asked, sitting at the kitchen table.

"He's in the den talking to Bill." Her mother pulled her chair closer to her. "How does Bill seem to you?"

Dana thought for a minute. "Okay, kind of. He's faraway acting, or something, but he's still the same Bill he was back home." She decided not to go into the reason why she had walked Trixie that morning. Bill probably just didn't feel like it.

"He always spends so much time in his room." Her mother absently pulled at her bottom lip.

"We just got here. He doesn't know anybody. What do you expect him to do?"

Her mother said, "Of course, you're right," but her expression was still thoughtful. "Maybe he's unpacking some of the cartons in his room."

"Maybe. I've still got three left myself."

Her mother seemed satisfied with that explanation.

Dana pointed at the computer. "I notice you unpacked *that* right away. What are you writing?"

Her face brightened. "I've been doing research for an article on the Hollywood Bowl. I thought I'd get some background before I drive over to see it."

"There's lots to write about around . . . "

All of a sudden, Clark McAllister's voice boomed from the den. "What do you mean you haven't sent in the college applications? We're late getting them in as it is because of the move. I go to all the trouble of picking them up for you and you don't fill them out?" Dana couldn't hear Bill's answer, but her father said, "What questions are funny? Those aren't personal questions. Nobody's prying. They *need* that information."

Dana felt something twist in her chest as though her father were "having a little talk" with *her*. Dad's cool and all, she thought, but sometimes there's no *talking* to him. He's all engineer with his numbers and measurements. But he didn't usually land *this* hard. What *was* going on with Bill?

Her mother said softly, "I think sometimes too much emphasis is put on schoolwork, but your father . . . "

Dana crumbled the granola wrapper into a tight ball. "I *hate* it when he lands on us like that. Doesn't he know we just *moved* here."

She still couldn't hear Bill, but heard her father yell, "When it comes to your future, they want to hear about grades, units, degrees, concrete performance. Now, you'd better get cracking, Bill, or you're going to foul up the most important school year of your life."

Dana wanted to burst in the room and shout, "Leave Bill alone." But she could never stand up to her father like that, so she jumped up, tossed the wrapper in the trash and leaned against the kitchen counter, scowling.

Her mother nodded her understanding, but didn't move.

Bill and her father talked a little longer, more quietly. It sounded almost like a good conversation to Dana. Then the den door opened. Dana watched her father come out and was surprised to see he wasn't wearing one of his "frowns of disappointment." Bill dashed up the wrought iron staircase without looking at anybody, his narrow face averted, his thin shoulders bent. Trixie ran from the room and bounded ahead of him.

Her father came into the kitchen, sighed, and said, "Bill and I had a good talk, Libby. I lost my temper a little because he's, well, preoccupied or something, but I really believe everything is going to be all right." He poured himself a mug of coffee and sat at the table. His gray hair streaking back from his temples and his black-rimmed glasses gave him a stern but distinguished look. "He's at a sensitive age, has just moved to the other side of the country, is worried about getting into college. Maybe everything caught up with him. After this talk, I think he'll get his priorities straight." He patted her shoulder. "It's just a stage." He sighed. "I'm sorry I lost it with him."

Her mother's shoulders relaxed and she smiled as though she'd been given a diamond ring. "It's good you had the talk, Clark."

As she got ready for bed that night, Dana decided this had been one of the best days of her life. She really liked the new school, and most of her teachers, and she had met some really cool kids. She rummaged in her pink plastic jewelry box for her rope and bead necklace. She wasn't going to worry about Bill anymore because her father said he was going through a stage, just a teenage stage. She folded her "Summer in Cape Cod" shirt over her chair and sat at her desk to paint her nails with the silver glitter polish Aunt Deb had given her when she moved from Boston.

CHAPTER TWO

Thursday, Dana was still sitting at the same lunch table. This day, as usual, the cafeteria was total chaos. Kids were talking, eating, shuffling around looking for seats. The noise was deafening, and the ceiling had so many fluorescent lights you could perform open heart surgery on one of the tables. That was Ian's joke.

As she left the cafeteria line with her two enchiladas and can of diet soda she glanced ahead at her table. Most of the kids who sat there were juniors, some were in her classes, or P.E. But Dana always looked for the ones she'd met the first day. Especially Eric Bergman.

She spotted him right away strolling toward the cafeteria line and noticed that half the girls in the room saw him, too. She hoped he would sit at the table. Sometimes he sat with the tennis kids. There was an empty seat across from Sheila and Joannie, next to Ian, so she took it. When Eric sat next to her, Dana tried not to stare at him but from the corner of her eye saw that the sleeves of his blue sweater were pushed up and golden hairs glistened on his tanned arms. The whole side of her body next to him prickled, even though they weren't touching. He's so gorgeous, she thought.

"How's it going?" he asked casually.

"Okay." Wouldn't it be nice, she thought, if someone gave us a script so that we'd always say the right thing. She blushed thinking of some of the dumb things she's said in her life, but felt safe with "okay."

Sheila wiped her fingers on a paper napkin and handed some papers she'd been reading to Joannie. "Why don't you just throw them out?"

"Show them around." Ian turned to Dana. "This guy sometimes passes out poems near the library and he gave some to Joannie."

Eric grabbed one of the poems. "Listen to this: 'Of green things and life, of rabbits and wren, from lack causing strife.' The guy's crazy."

"Shut up, Eric," Sheila said, pushing his arm.

Dana read a poem called "Skottr and Jjaim" that rambled on about Moses. "It isn't scary, really, just weird." She turned to Sheila. "Why did you tell her to throw them out?"

Sheila had an embarrassed expression as she concentrated on squeezing hot sauce on her taco. "Why not?" She shrugged.

"What do *you* think I should do?" Joannie asked Dana. "They make me nervous." Joannie wore a T-shirt with "Hollywood Star" printed across the front. Turquoise earrings hung from her ear lobes.

"It doesn't matter," Dana told her. "He passes them around to everyone, doesn't he?"

"I saw this guy one day in the mart buying gum. Later, I saw him shuffling along the road, talking to himself, waving his arms." Eric jumped up, waved his arms, and mumbled.

Dana giggled but then thought, Why does he do things like that? He's right and all, but still . . . . She squirmed and looked down.

Ian said, "If I see him I'll snap his picture for my 'California Characters' portfolio."

"What's that?" Dana asked.

"Oh, a collection of pictures I've taken of unusual people around here."

Eric said, "Somebody ought to snare him in the nut net and lock him up. He's crazy."

They were all looking at Eric so they were startled to hear Ian say, "It's no crime to be crazy." Ian was usually more of a listener than talker. "I don't know what you could lock him up for. Buying gum?" He held a dripping sandwich in midair.

Eric shrugged. "Because he writes crazy poems." He thought for a moment. "But maybe you're right."

"There are weird people all over the place," Ian said.

Dana said, "Sure, I remember a guy who used to dance at half time in the football field at Paul Revere High. He wore a long, wrinkled coat. We called him the mayor of Monkey Hill."

Eric hooted. "The mayor of Monkey Hill. That's great."

Joannie tossed her blond hair and scowled. "Weird people make me feel itchy."

"Oh, let's forget about the stupid poems," said Sheila. "Let's talk about the dance tomorrow night. Remember, it will be an eighties-type dance. I got a terrific "Flash Dance" poster of Jennifer Beals that's practically a collector's item."

"What about music?" asked Eric.

"My uncle has a CD with "Lady. Lady. Lady" and "Maniac" and "Gloria" . . . all the terrific pieces."

"Oh, great," said Joannie, cramming the poems into her empty milk container. "I'll have big hair like those girls I've seen pictures of." She bunched her hair over her head, grinning.

"I'd better get new batteries for my flash," Ian told himself.

"What dance?" asked Dana, feeling her face blush.

"The usual one, last Friday of the month after school in the gym," Ian told her. "You don't have to dress special."

"If you feel like dancing, just show up," Sheila said, leaving for the library.

When she was gone, Joannie whispered to Dana, "I hope she fixes *her* hair and doesn't come looking like a bag lady."

All the way home on the school bus, Dana wondered what it would be like to *dance* with Eric, actually touch him. What would she wear? She should have asked Joannie what shampoo she used. Maybe she'd try to curl her hair or something. Did kids in California dance the same way the kids in Boston danced? What if she couldn't dance *right*?

When she walked into the kitchen at five-thirty, Dana remembered that her parents were having dinner somewhere on Figueroa Street in Downtown L.A. with people her father worked with and wouldn't be home until late. Trixie had been left in the backyard so she let her in, grabbed a bag of corn chips and a grape juice and went up to her room. First, she wanted to go through her clothes to see what she'd wear. Then, she had a ton of math and science homework to do, and there were still three big cartons of stuff to unpack from the movers. She could hear Bill in his room, probably doing his homework, too, but she didn't bother him.

While she was finally working on the math, she realized the room was getting dark and she was getting hungry. Hours had gone by. Feeling her way through the darkening house, she turned on lights as she went down to the kitchen. She broiled two cheese, tomato, and mushroom pizzas on English muffins, with extra cheese, in case Bill wanted one.

As she was about to knock on his door, she heard a voice and stopped. She was sure it was Bill and not his radio, but who was he talking to? He's probably memorizing something by saying it out loud, she decided. But something in his voice made her stay outside the door. She heard him pacing, then, he laughed . . . not a what-a-funny-joke sort of laugh, but more of a private laugh.

She knocked on his door. Then, she knocked again.

After what seemed like a whole minute, he asked, "Did somebody knock?"

"It's me, Bill."

He opened the door.

"Oh, hi, Dane. Come on in." His breath smelled as though he hadn't brushed his teeth. He had a kind of distant expression on his face as if he'd been napping. She went in and sat on the edge of his bed.

Dana looked around. What was going on with his room? The photograph of Coach Loughlin with his old soccer team at Paul Revere was turned to the wall. His pillow was under the bed. Everywhere she looked something was *wrong*. She and Bill had always been private about their rooms, and they were expected to pick up their messes themselves, but this was more than a mess.

"Why do you have so many oranges?" she asked. There must have been a dozen oranges in a bowl, and the wastepaper basket was full of orange peels and seeds . . . full of them.

Bill stared at the fruit, opened his mouth, but didn't answer.

I'd better not ask any more questions, she decided.

"What's up?" he asked, sitting by his desk.

"Not much. School's not bad. How about you?"

He shrugged. "Okay."

Dana thought he looked sad sitting there, his arms hanging by his side. She wondered why the picture was turned around, but didn't say anything.

A part of her wanted to think about Eric and the dance and what to wear. She had decided on her new overall jeans, but now thought they might look dumb at an 80s dance. She wanted to go back to her room and didn't know what to say to her brother. Then she noticed his old telescope by the window.

"Bill, remember the night we tried to see astronauts on the moon? Remember you thought you could see people walking on the moon? You said you could even see their faces. Remember?"

He stood and stared out the window, up at the night sky. "I could," he whispered. "Just that one night, I know I could."

"But, you couldn't *really*. Even a scientist on Mount Palomar wouldn't be able to see *that* distinctly. Besides, you were only about thirteen. I remember because I had just had my eleventh birthday." Dana felt uneasy, but stayed on the edge of his bed anyway.

"You don't understand, Dane . . . about the sky, I mean. I've been looking at it a lot lately. And, well, there are things up there even the scientists don't know about."

"Like . . . what things?"

"Dane, I'm not imagining this. Come here and I'll prove something to you."

He pulled her over to the window and gave her the telescope. The sun had set and the night was clear and beautiful. The sliver of new moon hung low in the sky.

"See? Right about there." He directed the telescope toward a particular spot. "What do you see?"

Dana focused the lens but wasn't able to see anything except stars. The telescope wasn't even pointed toward the few things in the skies that were familiar to her, like the Big Dipper or Venus. "I don't know much about the sky." She was bewildered and a little frightened. His breath was warm on the back of her neck. *He's so really nervous because I'm not seeing what he wants me to see,* she thought. I'd better look again. "Is it the Milky Way? I can see that over this way a little." The night was so clear the Milky Way streaked across the sky like a distant snowstorm.

"Come on, Dane. Let me have it back." His hands trembled. He took the telescope and focused it. "Right where I'm pointing. See how those stars spell my name? B-I-L-L. I think someone is trying to get a message to my brain."

Her back felt as though a thousand worms were crawling on it. She took a step away from him. "Who?" she asked.

"That's just it, Dane. I can't figure anything out."

She wanted to scream. "You're crazy! You're nuts!" but stopped herself. Instead she said, "Let me look again, Bill. I don't really understand the sky like you do." She looked in the same direction he'd looked, afraid to upset him any more, and said, "Maybe I *can* see like a B."

But Bill was staring at the sky with a puzzled look on his face. He stared for a very long time. He didn't even turn when she left.

Dana went to her room. She put her cold pizza on her dresser next to a picture of Bill and her taken at Moosehead Lake in Maine about seven years earlier.

She thought of the great time they'd had together that summer . . . fishing, swimming, water skiing. In the afternoons, she and Bill rowed over to a small island to pick wild blueberries. He'd clown around and rock the boat, pretending to dump her. He was fun. Then, in the evenings Mom, Dad, Bill, and she would sit by the lake eating lobsters, roasted potatoes, fresh corn, and the blueberries. They'd sit for hours, talking, watching the moon come up, listening to the loons screaming far out on the lake. Bill was okay then. Dana studied the face of the skinny-legged young boy in swim trunks and sneakers grinning at her from the picture. He was just a regular kid. Now, he was . . . she didn't know what. A coldness ran across her shoulders.

A part of her was mad at Bill because she didn't want to think about him and his wacky ideas about the sky. She wanted to think about Eric, the dance, what she'd wear and what she'd say.

She did her homework as best she could, put the overalls back in her closet and pulled out her regular jeans, and went to bed. When her parents came home, she pretended to be asleep.

In the middle of the night, she woke once. Down the hall, she heard Bill pacing in his room.

CHAPTER THREE

Next morning, Dana woke with the awful feeling something was wrong. Why? Her first thought was of the dance that afternoon. She should feel happy. She tried to remember, her mind still half asleep.

Then, it came back to her. Something *was* wrong... with Bill. She lay curled in her warm bed, her patchwork quilt tucked under her chin, wondering what to tell her parents.

Trixie padded around the hallway, sniffing under doors, probably wishing someone would get up and start the day. She usually slept at the top of the staircase on a rag rug. After a while, Dana heard her father start the shower and her mother go down the stairs to the kitchen, Trixie yelping in delight. Dad's got that engineer's conference in Santa Monica today, Dana remembered. Maybe I'll wait until he's gone and talk to Mom. Then she remembered that the literature group her mother had joined was going to a theater party at the Dorothy Chandler Pavilion in the afternoon. She hated to wreck her day.

Dana rolled on her back and put her hands under her head. For some reason, things didn't look so bad now that morning had come. She closed her eyes and pictured D-A-N-A in the stars. Sure, anyone could see all kinds of words in the sky. Maybe this was what Dad called Bill's "extraordinary imagination."

She got out of bed and pulled on a pink terry robe. Maybe it wouldn't be fair to betray Bill's confidence, anyhow. He wouldn't do that to *me*, she thought. She brushed her teeth, showered and was creaming her face with the vitamin E and nasturtium lotion that Joannie recommended when her father shouted from the bottom of the stairs.

"Good-bye, Dana. I'm off to the conference. Wish me luck driving on the Santa Monica Freeway."

She ran to the landing. "So long, Dad. See you later." When her mother was back from walking Trixie, Dana went downstairs, wondering why her father hadn't shouted goodbye to Bill. Her mother was stirring apple slices and raisins in a fry pan and smiled weakly as Dana came into the kitchen. Her mother wore white shorts and a yellow shirt, but still hadn't brushed her hair.

"Where's Bill, Mom?"

"He, uh, he left early."

Dana noted the hesitation in her mother's answer. She poured herself a mug of Guatemalan coffee from the coffeemaker, then stood in the middle of the floor sipping it, wondering what to say.

Her mother sprinkled cinnamon in the pan, her lips tight. "I think he's doing okay, Dana. I think he's trying."

"Mom." She still wondered what to say.

"He told Dad he's going to join the soccer team *and* the astronomy club."

"Mom."

"Believe it or not, he actually changed his shirt." She gave a kind of half laugh.

"Mom, he's got a thousand oranges in his room."

"Oranges?" She looked bewildered and opened the refrigerator door. "He must have taken that big bag of them upstairs." She shook her head. "They're too messy to eat in a bedroom. What's the matter with him?"

Dana couldn't let that go. "Something is, Mom. He's, I don't know what, weird or something." She knew there was a better word but didn't know what it was.

Her mother switched off the burner, took the fry pan off the hot coils, and turned to face her. Dana saw a truly worried look on her mother's face. "You don't think he's gotten into drugs, do you, Dana?"

Dana shook her head. "I thought of that, too, but I really don't think so. I really don't." She just didn't think Bill would do something that stupid.

Her mother pointed to her computer. "I thought maybe he was depressed and even looked the word up on the Internet, but that didn't seem . . . " She shook her head, her arms limp by her side.

Dana glanced at the wall clock. She had to get dressed or she'd miss the school bus. "Maybe it *is* nothing, Mom. I mean nothing serious . . . just moving and new school and being eighteen."

Her mother put her hands on Dana's shoulders and kissed her on the forehead. "I'm glad you came downstairs. At least, we've talked about it." Her expression was solemn. "Your father doesn't seem to see what you and I see."

Dana decided to leave cheerful. "Don't worry, Mom. If he's joining the astronomy club, he's okay."

Later, waiting at the bus stop, Dana was glad she hadn't told her mother about the telescope and Bill's name in the stars. You could probably read the Declaration of Independence up there if you wanted to. Still, she was really glad that she had talked to her mother and hoped they'd worried for nothing. If Bill went to school, she thought, he's probably fine. She was tired of thinking about him.

She wanted to think about Eric and the dance.

When Dana walked into the dance that afternoon, the gym was already half full. Mats and equipment had been pushed into one corner. Chairs brought in from the cafeteria lined the sides. She stood against the wall for a moment, smiling a stiff smile, scanning the dancers for Eric, but couldn't see him. Kids milled around, stood around, hung around, and danced around.

Dana felt self-conscious. She spotted Sheila in jeans and a man's shirt, standing on a chair hanging her "Flash Dance" poster, her mouth full of thumbtacks. She's always so helpful, Dana thought. Plus she's got something to *do*. She doesn't have to stand around feeling dumb.

"The room really has the look of the 80s," Dana told her, pointing to other posters. "You found "Duran Duran" and "Madonna" and that's "U2," isn't it?"

"Yeah," said Sheila, now rearranging soda cans and plastic bottles of water in a tub of ice. "It was for 'The Joshua Tree' album."

"They were really popular back in Boston because so many Irish Americans live there."

Dana glanced around surreptitiously. Ian stood in the corner talking to some kids, his camera case hanging from his shoulder. Probably always looking for a character for his album, she thought. Dana stood next to Sheila and watched the dancers while the stereo blared "I Love Rock and Roll." "They're dancing about the same as we did in Boston," she joked.

"Oh, they can dance any way they want."

Why does she say "they" instead of "we," Dana wondered? Doesn't she even *plan* to dance? "Well, Joannie sure knows how. Look." Dana pointed to the center of the dance floor.

Joannie in red leg warmers danced with one of the football players, her suddenly curly, curly hair bobbing to the beat.

Sheila said, "Joannie can show you everything you want to know about being happy."

Dana returned to surveying the room as casually as she could. The breath caught in her throat when she saw Eric stroll into the gym. "What was the score?" he called to kids on the basketball team. He waved to someone behind Dana but didn't seem to see her. Then he turned and went up to a girl with dark curly hair who had just come in.

Sheila said, "Half the girls in the room would *die* just to have Eric *look* at them."

"I know. He's so popular and everything." When she saw him dance onto the floor with the dark-haired girl, Dana went over to some kids in her history class who were standing the other side of the gym. Some of them were working on the yearbook after school and she'd been thinking of joining them.

A U2 song was nearly over—"I Still Haven't Found What I'm Looking For—" when she heard moans of "Oh, no!"

"What's wrong?" she asked the girl next to her.

"It's awful. Sheila's got her favorite disco record. Now we'll *all* have to get out and freestyle disco whether we feel like it or not. She plays it *every time*."

Dana moaned "Oh, no" along with the others but was secretly grateful for the opportunity to *have* to dance. She joined the million kids dancing in the middle of the floor, but not before seeing that

Eric was there as well. Pretending she didn't know what direction she was going in, Dana moved closer to him. He was just over to her left dancing with a girl who was smiling up at him as if he had a plan for saving the ozone. Dana's heart beat faster. She half wished she wore leg warmers, too, instead of jeans and her Cape Cod T-shirt or had her hair pulled over in a stretchy like girls in the 80s.

Suddenly, she was next to Eric. "How's it goin'?" he asked, winking down at her.

"Great!" A pulse drummed in her temple. "Really great." The music kept playing. Dana kept dancing, hoping the glitter she had put on her cheeks hadn't worn off.

Eric turned to face her, dancing so close she smelled the wonderful soap and wool-sweater smell of him. He brushed her shoulder with his arm as he danced and the whole side of her body tingled. Then "Pretty cool, Dana, pretty cool," and he was gone, smiling his amazing smile over her head, toward someone behind her . . . not at her. She stayed on the floor until the dance ended, remembering how she had felt when he was close to her, wishing he would come back. But he never did. Next time she saw him he was demonstrating a tennis serve to rapt watchers.

Dana stood against the wall again, but only for a minute. I can't stand around like a tree, she thought. I wish I were home. As she tried to calm herself she thought, there I was *dancing* with him and couldn't think of anything to *say*. Smiling too brightly, she went down the hall to the girls' room. She leaned against the cool tile wall a moment, then washed her face, smoothed her hair over her ears, took a deep breath, and returned to the dance. The music had changed. Sheila had put on one of her tapes from the 40s as a joke, a Glenn Miller called, "String of Pearls."

"I'm willing to try, if you are." Ian stood next to her, pointing to the dance floor. "But I don't have a clue how to dance like that."

"I don't either," Dana giggled.

That didn't stop them. Out they went.

"We're terrible!" Dana laughed. "We can't get the beat."

Every time Ian spun her out, she crashed back into his arms. And his camera case kept bashing into her shoulder.

"If I put it down, I might miss the picture of the century."

It was then that Eric danced into view. "You have to learn to dip," he told them, bending his dance partner, a willowy redhead with lavender eye shadow, far back.

"What did I tell you? I can't miss this one." Click went Ian's camera.

Click. He took a picture of the girl.

When the music stopped, Ian said, "Thanks, that's all for me," and walked Dana off the dance floor. "There's a definite lack of coordination on this floor." And he wandered off.

She talked again with kids in her history class for a while and when the dance ended, joined the line at the phone booth. Maybe one of her parents was home and could pick her up. Otherwise, she'd take the Friday night dance bus.

"Need a ride? I'm going past Lemon Grove anyway." Ian stood next to her organizing stuff in his camera case.

"Sure. Thanks."

"I think I got some good shots," he told her as they walked toward his blue Mustang. "Black and white . . . that's the best kind for indoors at night; 35mm slides for daylight." On the drive home he explained cameras to her. "I like to catch people when they're not posing. Someday I'll show you my portfolio. I have almost twenty-five pictures."

As Ian turned the corner into her street, Dana noticed bright lights up ahead. "What's going on?" she asked. "Is that a police car?"

"It looks like a fire truck, no, an ambulance," said Ian, slowing the car.

She squinted up the block. "Oh, no, I think it's in front of my house. Something's happened . . . maybe to my brother." Her heart pounded. "He's been feeling, like, sick or something."

"I didn't know you had a brother."

"Yes, he's . . . he's . . . over in the senior annex."

Ian parked the car wherever he could and grabbed his camera. "Oh, no," Dana pleaded, "please, don't take pictures. *Please!*"

"I'm sorry. It's just a habit." He looked surprised but hid the camera under the front seat and locked the car doors.

They ran across the street together. When they got into the house, Dana heard her mother scream, "Bill, stop it! STOP IT! Listen to me!"

Bill ran over to Dana. "Help me!" He looked wild, frightened. "Listen, Dane," he said, grabbing her arm. "Bugs are biting me all over. I don't know where they're coming from."

Once again, she thought . . . he must be on some drug, but still didn't believe it.

A man about twenty-five, average height, in white shirt and trousers, stood next to Bill talking quietly to him.

"Take it easy, now. My name is Victor and my partner here is Artie." His voice was low, soothing. "We'll help you figure it out." Dana thought that Artie looked as big as a sumo wrestler.

"What happened?" Dana demanded, running up to her mother.

"Oh, I'm so glad to see you. I didn't know what to do. Nobody was home. You were at the dance. There was no answer at the school. Dad's at the conference. I tried to call him. No one could find him. I don't know any of the neighbors. I didn't know what to do." She held the side of her head with one hand and gripped Dana's arm with the other.

Dana glanced out the front door at the ambulance and police car. Neighbors stood in doorways or watched from their windows, but couldn't see into the house. Suddenly, she was embarrassed, mad even. Why couldn't Bill act normal instead of . . . like this.

Artie moved behind Bill who was pacing frantically, his head down, lost in some weird thought.

Her mother tried to explain. "He kept running back and forth in his room and all over the house, up and down the stairs," she whispered. "He's so strong, I didn't know how to stop him. I was afraid he'd run out in the street and get killed. So I called the police, and they came with these men."

Artie said, "We're called the PMRT."

Ian asked, "What does that mean?"

Victor said, "Psychiatric Mobile Response Team." He never took his eyes off Bill.

Artie added, importantly, "We're trained to handle this sort of situation."

Bill started talking again. "It's because of the pictures on my walls. Remember the one with Coach Loughlin? He keeps telling me to eat oranges so that my skin won't turn blue. Orange is the opposite of blue on the color wheel. You know that, Dane."

Dana shivered. All those oranges in his room were for *that* reason? She looked around. Where was Ian? Then, she saw him standing by a policeman who was handing a piece of paper to Victor. "I wrote you a 5150. Where you takin' him?"

"Parson's has a bed."

Dana ran over. "What's a 5150?" She looked, anxiously, from the policeman to Victor to Ian.

The policeman said, "This'll put a hold on him for 72 hours, give a doctor a chance to make an evaluation, see what you're dealing with." He jiggled his keys. "He'll do fine at Parson's," he told Dana and her mother and left.

Artie had gone outside and now was wheeling a gurney through the front door.

Dana heard Victor tell her in a low voice, "first, we've got to get him on this, then into the ambulance . . . "

Get him into the ambulance? Then, Dana realized what was going to happen. These men were going to take Bill away.

CHAPTER FOUR

Dana's throat tightened. She ran over to her brother, "It'll be okay. Oh, Bill, it'll be okay." She shivered, although the air was warm.

Ian now stood next to Bill, silent but alert.

Bill became more and more agitated. "Don't touch me!" he screamed. "I'll break. My bones are dissolving." All of a sudden, it looked as though he might run out of the house—just run and run. All Dana could think of was that he might even run right over to Tanoble Drive, up into the San Gabriel mountains and get lost forever.

Artie shut the front door to keep Bill inside.

Suddenly, her mother cried out. "Don't hurt him."

Dana threw her body against Bill's to shield him. She couldn't bear to see him so frightened and vulnerable. Victor pulled her gently away, and she stood sobbing into her hands.

Dana heard Ian say, "I'm sorry, Bill." He was trying to hold the gurney steady for Victor and Artie.

Her mother stood against the wall, her hand to her mouth, her eyes brimming with tears. "Dear God, help him."

It took the strength of both men to finally get Bill strapped down on the gurney, all the time telling him "this is so you can't hurt yourself, kid."

Bill struggled against the restraints, sobbing, "Mom, Dane, help me!"

"There," said Victor, "Let's get him out to the van."

"*Where are you taking him?*" Dana screamed.

"Please, wait," her mother said. "I'll follow you. *Wait.* I have to find my car keys." She stumbled toward the kitchen.

Ian stood before Dana with his head bowed. "Is there anything I can do?"

"No, please, Ian, just go. Thanks a lot—really—but please, just go."

He nodded. "I'll call you tomorrow." Then he added, "I'm sorry, Dana."

As she watched Ian walk toward his car she thought, was it really only tonight when I danced with him? Her stunned brain wouldn't let her think any further.

All the way down, her mother drove, bent forward, her eyes fixed on the red taillights in front of her.

Dana didn't dare speak because she didn't want to break her mother's concentration, but all she could think was that nothing like this had ever happened in her family before. Bill had acted as if someone else's brain had been put in his skull. What was wrong with him?

Finally, the ambulance sped onto the 210 freeway, exited on Santa Anita, then roared all the way down to the city of El Monte. Dana made careful note of the route as they turned onto a side street in kind of a rundown neighborhood of boarded up stores where it stopped by a yellow and black neon sign reading "Parson's Hospital—Emergency." Dana thought the building looked more like offices than a hospital. By the time her mother found a parking spot in the visitor's section, Victor had already wheeled Bill inside. Artie spotted Dana and her mother hurrying toward the emergency room door and pointed toward the front of the building, shouting, "Why don't you go to the admitting office and see about the paperwork while we take your brother inside."

"Where are you going with him?" Dana asked.

"We'll have someone take a look at him, make an evaluation, and be back to you in no time." He looked at Dana. "And you'd better hang on to your mother. She doesn't look so good."

It was then Dana realized her mother was clinging to her arm, her pale face motionless. Dana reached for her mother's purse, hanging like a weight from her hand and led her toward admitting.

"What's going on, Dana?" Her expression was intense as she

fixed on the emergency room door Bill had disappeared through. "It's okay, Mom." Dana patted her mother's arm. She seemed to be saying that a lot . . . and it didn't make sense.

The main lobby had several comfortable couches and chairs, a table with magazines and a small gift shop. Dana was only half aware that people were sitting around as she followed the signs to the admitting office. A middle age man, with an official looking badge on his shirt pocket reading Josef, seemed to be patrolling the hallway. Dana wondered if he was an off-duty policeman. He nodded cordially to them as they entered a small office, painted bright yellow, with pictures of sunsets and flowers on the walls. A lady with curly gray hair sat at a desk and motioned them to sit down. "My name is Ruth," she said, cheerfully. "How can I help you?"

"It's my brother, Bill. He came in with the ambulance."

"I see. Now, why not let me have all the particulars. It's beyond belief the number of forms that have to be filled out these days. We might as well get started. First of all, has he been here before?"

"No, never," Dana answered, shocked.

"May I ask what kind of insurance you have?"

Her mother turned a blank face to Dana.

"Maybe you've got a card in your purse," Dana said, and then, to Ruth, "We just moved here from Massachusetts."

"We're only half unpacked." Her mother picked through her wallet and finally handed Ruth a plastic card.

Ruth took down the information. "I'm pretty sure this policy will cover you here in California." She turned the card over and wrote down some numbers. "Pretty sure."

Suddenly her mother's muddled look cleared. 'He might have a *fever*. Of course. That can make people delirious." She half rose from her chair. "I want to tell them to take his temperature."

"They probably will anyway." Dana answered, absently. A fever didn't seem likely to her.

"Spell his name, please," Ruth asked. "And I'll need your address and phone number." She punched a few buttons on her computer and a fresh form appeared on the screen.

Dana leaned forward and answered Ruth's questions.

Her mother murmured, "I was holding together fine, now . . . I feel as though I could shake to pieces." To Ruth she said, "Could we possibly use your phone to call home? I left my cell phone in the kitchen, charging."

Ruth nodded.

Dana dialed their number, let it ring twelve times, and shook her head.

"Maybe this will all be settled and we'll be home before your father," her mother hoped. So did Dana.

All of a sudden, a woman with an RN pin on the pocket of her plaid shirt came into the office and spoke in a low voice to Ruth. "A seventy-two-hour observation," she said, pointing to the paperwork. Her dark hair was pulled back with a rubberband.

Ruth nodded.

Dana's heart jumped in her chest when she heard the nurse say, "Mrs. McAllister?" She pointed to her badge. "My name is Elena. Dr. Wolzak, who is on duty tonight, has given Bill a mild tranquilizer to make him feel calmer because he's having problems with delusions . . . "

"Dr. who?" her mother asked.

"Dr. Wolzak, but Bill will be assigned a regular doctor tomorrow. It's too late this evening. Meantime, . . . "

Her mother looked over Elena's shoulder toward the doorway. "Can we talk to Dr. Wolzak?"

"He'll be out in a moment. We've had several emergencies . . . one of the other nurses had a car breakdown and . . . well." She threw up her hands and smiled cheerfully but Dana thought she looked harried.

"He'll be out as soon as he can," she repeated, and left.

Her mother continued to watch the doorway and jumped when the doctor finally came in the office with Bill at his side. Dana and her mother ran over to him. No one spoke for a moment, then Dana felt a sudden surge of affection and asked, "Are you okay?"

Bill nodded, standing docile as a child.

Dr. Wolzak was about fifty, lean, very tall with angular features. Dana thought he looked handsome in his white jacket and rimless glasses, but tired. He introduced himself, shaking hands with Dana and her mother. He carried a clipboard.

"When can Bill come home?" her mother asked first thing.

"Mrs. McAllister, we feel that he would benefit from a period of observation." He smiled toward Bill who sat on the edge of a chair by the door, nodding groggily.

Dana asked, "What do you think is wrong?"

Dr. Wolzak told her, "It's too soon to say. There are some tests we'd like to run first, lab work to be drawn, X-rays to take, perhaps a CAT scan or MRI, social workers to see, nurses to do evaluations, a doctor to be assigned." He spread his hands as if to emphasize all that had to be done.

"Do you know which doctor it will be?" her mother asked.

"No. No, I don't because I don't know my colleagues' schedules, but you'll be notified very soon." He removed a sheet of paper from his clipboard and handed it to her mother. "Meantime, may I ask you to fill out this brief family history form? You can give it to Ruth when you've finished. She'll have some others for you to fill out, I'm sure."

Dana looked over at Bill who was rubbing his arms again. "He thinks bugs are all over him," she told Dr. Wolzak.

"So he tells me."

Dana saw him glance at his watch and knew the meeting was over.

"Well, we'll get to the bottom of it," he assured them.

"I hope so," her mother told him.

He shook hands all around again, promised they'd take good care of Bill and was gone.

Outside Ruth's office he spoke to the guard, "Busy day, Josef?"

"Had busier," Josef answered, politely.

"Have a young man in Ruth's office with his family."

"I'm aware."

"Tom will be out in just a moment. We had an emergency . . ."

"I'm aware."

Dana sat next to Bill while her mother read through a form. "How are you doing?" she asked, bending to look into his face.

His speech was slurred, but he clearly meant what he said, "It's true about the coach, Dane." He stared at a painting of flowers over Ruth's desk as if his coach's face was in them.

She shivered and fell silent.

Then Ruth said, "We need more information, Bill. What's your social security number?"

Dana was surprised to hear him give her the number, slowly but accurately. How can he remember his social security number and still have crazy ideas about his coach, she wondered?

Finally, Ruth was finished and printed out form after form.

"Mrs. McAllister, why don't you look these over? As I warned you, there's enough of them—insurance forms, medical history forms, forms giving permission for various tests—on and on." She pointed. "If you would sign where I have highlighted the various spots . . . "

This is really awful, thought Dana.

Her mother half-rose from her chair, picked up her purse and said, "I want to take Bill home."

"See? Look at him!" said Dana to Ruth. "He's all right now." But she knew she had said it to back up her mother. Of course, he wasn't all right. He just brushed more bugs off his shoulder.

Ruth said, "The hospital can only keep him for seventy-two hours against his will. That's the law. That's what the 5150 was for. It authorized the PMRT men to bring him here for observation." She paused. "Now, I must tell you that seventy-two hours does not count a weekend, so tomorrow and Sunday won't count." She went on. "After that, they can keep him an additional two weeks if a doctor thinks it's necessary." She shrugged. "After that . . . "

Her mother stiffened.

"And, don't forget," Ruth went on, "he has only been given a tranquilizer and when that wears off, he'll still feel the way he did earlier." She looked over at him. "What do you think, Bill? Do you want to spend some time here?"

Bill slowly raised his head, an awful look of sadness on his face, and whispered, "Yes."

Dana gasped.

Her mother didn't cry. She turned in her chair, looked a long time into Bills' face, then slowly nodded.

After her mother had signed the last form, Ruth made a phone call. Pretty soon a man in his twenties, dressed casually in chinos and short-sleeved shirt, came into the room. He was short, heavy and wore three silver earrings in his right ear. His name tag read "Tom." Ruth handed him some of the paperwork and pointed to Bill. "Tom, this is Bill McAllister."

Tom went over. "How ya' doin'?"

Bill stood, and so did Dana and her mother. "One of the staff doctors will be in touch with you," Tom told them.

"Can't we phone Bill?" asked Dana, realizing at once that he wasn't going home with them.

"Sure can."

Bill had already walked to the door and stood staring at the ground, his foot raised as though still watchful for bugs to squash.

Dana asked Ruth, "What's the phone number here."

Ruth handed her a brochure, pointing out visiting hours and telephone numbers.

Dana searched in vain for something sensible to say, but her mind was empty.

Tom leaned toward her. His voice was gentle when he said, "Your brother will be fine here."

Dana noticed people kept saying that to her.

Ruth pushed a buzzer, and Bill and Tom went through a thick glass door that shut and locked behind them.

Dana raced to the door, rapped as hard as she could, and shouted, "Bill, listen. I'll take care of Trixie. Everything will be fine." She was saying it, too.

But Bill continued walking down the corridor.

Dana watched until they turned a corner out of sight. Still she stood, looking around. She saw a man in pajamas talking into a pay phone, crying. A girl around seventeen sat at a table in the dark, not moving. Who else is in there? Dana wondered. She felt numb. Behind her, Josef said, "He'll be fine."

Her mother drove the car home slowly, taking the back roads. By the time they got there, Dana felt sick to her stomach and her mother's right eyelid twitched.

"I'll be okay," she told Dana, pouring a glass of ice water from the fridge. "I'll lie on the couch until your father comes home."

Upstairs, Dana lay on her bed, glad to be alone. Her mind darted from one event of the day to another as though someone were showing her a different slide every second. From all the thoughts whirling in her head, one finally stayed with her. Bill was in a mental hospital and not down the hall in his own room. Those men in that ambulance had decided he had to go there. What was worse, Bill had admitted himself.

Dana turned on her side and pulled the covers over her head as a thought her brain had not let her think before now came to the front. "What's everybody going to think?" Remember how Eric and Joannie had talked about the man who gave out the poems at the library, how would they feel about her if they knew what had happened tonight? They have such perfect lives, Dana thought, Eric and Joannie. They're good-looking, smart, popular, dressed right. Nothing ever seemed to go wrong for them. Dana felt envy and didn't like the feeling. Her pillow was damp with tears.

Maybe I won't be sitting at the lunch table anymore, she thought, realizing she'd had a taste of the "in" group for exactly a month. Even Sheila, who wasn't really part of the "in" group, just sat at the table sometimes, didn't seem to like to talk about people who weren't "regular."

Dana was thankful that at least it was only Ian who had seen anything.

But what if he tells everybody?

CHAPTER FIVE

Dana awoke from a deep sleep to the sound of her father shouting downstairs in the living room. She bolted upright in bed. Moonlight streamed through her window onto her clock—almost midnight.

"What do you mean, you *had* to put him in the hospital?"

Dana couldn't hear her mother's answer, so she climbed out of bed and padded across the soft rug to the door.

Her father went on. "I can't believe you couldn't reason with him."

Now their voices came from the kitchen. Her father was on the phone. "You don't understand. My son doesn't *belong* down there. Is a Dr. Wolzak still on duty?" There was a pause. "Could he kindly call me?" Dana heard the phone slammed down. Then, "I just can't believe this, Libby. The way computers are these days, a record like this could follow him through the rest of his life."

Shivering, Dana pulled on her pink terry robe and went downstairs. Her mother would never be able to make him understand, she thought. He was just too stubborn, too blind to either of his children's faults or weaknesses—too scared, maybe.

Her mother sat at the kitchen table nervously twisting a tin of black tea, while the kettle whistled its cap off. Her father stood by the refrigerator, scowling, barely acknowledging Dana's entrance. She turned off the burner and said, "Honest, Dad, you can't imagine what it was like. I went to the hospital with Mom and we had a terrible time."

He glared at her through black-rimmed glasses, shaking his head all the time.

"Dad, please try to understand. It's hard for *me* to believe what happened and I was here, but Dad, it was . . . "

"This is unspeakable." Her father's voice was bitter. His hands clutched each other. "My *son in a mental hospital.*"

How haggard Mom looks, just staring at the tin of tea, Dana thought. She tried again. "You don't understand, Dad. Bill was really acting weird. He thought Coach Loughlin told him to eat *oranges.* He thought bugs were biting him. Nobody could control him. The ambulance men had a lot of trouble just *holding* him." She decided not to add "strapping him on a gurney."

Dana felt tears spring up in her eyes and bit her lip to hold them back. I look so dumb when I cry, she thought. I can never convince anybody of anything. But she had to make him see the truth. "It was awful. All the neighbors were standing out there or looking through windows, wondering what was going on, and Bill was so wild and crazy. *We had no choice,*" she shouted, then burst into tears.

"All right, Dana. That's enough. I appreciate what you're trying to do, but Bill is an extremely brilliant boy under a lot of stress and you're making a mental case out of him."

Suddenly, her mother looked up at him. Her voice was low and she spoke slowly. "You weren't here. He was having delusions. He was hallucinating. He was frantic with dread of heaven-knows-what. He would have run clear across the country to get away from those insects." She paused and looked directly into his eyes. "I even searched his room for drugs when I got home. That's how bad he was." She lowered her voice and sighed. "Something's wrong with Bill and we've got to find out what. This has been coming on. I know that now. Even back home he was, I don't know, withdrawn or something. I think the move has triggered something." She paused. "I won't be an ostrich about this."

Dana was surprised to see her father flinch. She'd never seen her mother stand up to him before.

Her mother stood up. She still wore the beige silk dress she'd worn to the theater, only now it hung funny on her shoulders and wrinkles creased the back. "I've got to get some sleep, Clark. I can't take much more tonight. I want to be able to face Bill tomorrow without falling apart. I think I'll just go to bed."

"Well, there's not much more that can be said tonight, that's for sure." He picked up his jacket and headed out of the kitchen.

Her mother turned the kitchen lights off, picked up her shoes, and climbed wearily up the staircase.

Dana followed, her eyes still red.

Her father said, "I'm going to sit in the den for a while. Maybe the doctor will call, but I doubt it." He went to the bottom of the staircase, "Libby, I suppose you did what you had to, but I sure wish you'd waited."

Her mother only nodded.

"I want to go down with you tomorrow," Dana told her mother when they got upstairs. "And everything will be okay," she added, because it was the only dumb thing she could think of to say.

Late that night, Dana awoke to hear her parents arguing in their room. Her mother's voice floated through the open window. "I'm not accusing you of making Bill sick, Clark, but you *do* push them too hard sometimes." She was surprised to hear her father's answer. "Well, if I'm going to get blamed for Bill, can I get credit for Dana?" Credit? For me? Is Dad proud of me? Dana wondered, as she drifted back to sleep.

Next morning, Dana woke early. Usually, she slept late on weekends, but her mind started racing immediately.

Trixie sniffed under her door, making whiny sounds. Dana knew she should dress and walk the little dog, but her mind skipped to the night before. Poor Bill. What kind of night did he have? What kind of room had he slept in? Did he have a roommate? Who was *in* places like that, anyhow? Parson's sure hadn't looked the way she'd always imagined a mental hospital; it wasn't spooky looking, not a big stone building on top of a dark mountain with lunatics screaming through barred windows. Still, she didn't like thinking that Bill was down there. She was half afraid to visit him, but half exhilarated by the thought of it, too.

Trixie yipped again so Dana jumped out of bed, pulled on jeans, running shoes, and an old gray jacket with a hood, and ran downstairs. At the kitchen door, Trixie ran in circles while Dana tried to clip her leash on.

Outside, the chilly morning air stung her face. She didn't feel like running so she just walked along, thinking. She passed the hibiscus and bougainvillea, but the flowers didn't look as bright as usual. The birds of paradise seemed to droop. She walked about half a block toward Mendocino, Trixie pulling on the leash. Then suddenly she thought, I shouldn't have come out. I want to be home. No, I want to be back in the old house where everybody knew us. I could tell friends what happened. I don't know anybody here.

She turned to run, but too late. A lady she'd pass some mornings came down her driveway in her bathrobe and fuzzy slippers. Dana pulled up the hood of her jacket, but the woman came right out into the road.

"I noticed you had some excitement last night. Is everything all right?" She stepped closer. "I know it's none of my business. You just moved in and all . . . "

Dana stood frozen.

"An ambulance is always . . . what I mean to say is . . . if someone is sick . . . I'd like to help . . . if I could."

"It's okay." Dana knew that was her standard dumb thing to say.

"I don't mean to pry . . . I couldn't really see anything . . . but don't you have a brother?"

How could she say no. She nodded.

"Well, what I mean to say is . . . he's not *dangerous*, is he?"

Dana caught her breath as the awful idea hit her. Dangerous? Bill dangerous? "Of *course* not," she said, feeling anger flair in her eyes. She wanted to run home.

The woman picked up her newspaper and headed up her driveway. Then, she turned and added, "I understand some people have good luck with this new 'tough love.' Kids soon straighten out."

All of a sudden Dana felt as though everyone on the block was peeking at her from behind closed windows. Did anyone else think

Bill was dangerous? Bill? She ran all the way home, her heart thumping. She played in the backyard with Trixie for a while to quiet herself so that her mother wouldn't see how upset she was. "I hate California," she told the little dog.

In the kitchen, her mother stood at the sink squeezing grapefruit. Dana noticed that the computer screen was blank and wondered when her mother would be able to write again. She handed Dana a glass of juice. "You'll need breakfast," she said, absently.

Her father came downstairs rubbing his eyes. Glum, he poured a cup of coffee and sat in the rocker, his elbows on his knees, staring into the cup. Fortunately, Dr. Wolzak *had* phoned back the night before, expressed his concern about Bill and gone over the tests he felt should be done. Her father did seem to have mellowed a little, but was still determined to get Bill out, no matter what a seventy-two hour hold meant.

"If we leave here at nine-thirty, we'll get there a little before ten. I just want to get this idiotic situation settled."

"Would you like some eggs?" Dana saw hurt in her mother's eyes.

He shook his head and sat sometimes reading, sometimes just turning the pages of the *Pasadena Star News*.

The three hardly spoke on the ride to the hospital. Inside, a different woman buzzed the thick glass door open for them and a different guard was on duty. Obviously, Ruth and Josef didn't work day *and* night. Dana's skin prickled as she walked into the corridor Bill had disappeared down the night before. A young man and woman, both wearing T-shirts that read "You're okay," sat behind a desk facing a large reception area where people watched television, played ping pong, played board games, or sat on couches talking, or just sitting. The woman, whose name was Rosa, had a rose tattooed on her cheek. A thick blond braid decorated with tiny bows hung down her back. The man's wavy black hair was pulled back into a pony tail.

"What room is Bill McAllister in?" her father asked Rosa.

"Let's see here." Rosa traced her finger down the names on a printed list. "Do you have McAllister, Juan?" she asked the man.

"One thirty-nine," he answered, pointing. "I think he's in there. I know he's back from the lab and X-ray."

"We try to schedule meetings and tests and stuff for the hours when visitors aren't here," Rosa explained, cheerfully.

Dana noticed that Rosa wore at least eight power bracelets of different colors.

She winked when she saw Dana looking at her arm. "I don't want to miss any happiness, opportunity, or good luck."

"Have any of the tests come back?" her mother asked.

"Too soon." Juan told her.

As they walked in the direction Juan had pointed, Dana peered cautiously into the rooms. They look like motel rooms, she thought, noticing that the curtains and bedspreads were bright colors. In most of the rooms, people lay on beds or sat quietly in chairs. In one, a man sat on the edge of his bed. His pajama top was buttoned crooked and he wore only one slipper. At the end of the hallway, two women in cotton dresses and bare, white legs shook their heads over a jigsaw puzzle set up on a card table.

When Dana and her parents walked into room 139, Bill lay on a bed in his clothes, facing the wall. Dana bent to see if his eyes were open or closed. She could hardly keep from poking him awake in fun, but remembered the Bill of the night before and stopped. Her father went up to him. "Bill," he said, moving to the foot of the bed and bending over to look into his face. "I got down here as fast as I could." He leaned over further. "Bill, please, turn around and *look* at me. I want to get you out of this place. I'm sorry I wasn't home when all this happened."

"Maybe he's really asleep," Dana whispered.

Her mother touched Bill's shoulder. He jumped a little. "I've been worrying about you all night. Have you had any breakfast? There's a machine in the hall with milk and sandwiches. Would you like something?"

Slowly, Bill turned over and stared at her, his arm across his forehead, his face flat.

Dana wondered if they'd given him another shot, he acted so wiped out. Still, his eyes didn't have a droopy look, just sad.

"We were told lab work was done and X-rays taken. Have you talked to anyone; anyone been in to see you?"

Bill thought. "That doctor from last night, some other doctor that's been in a couple of times, I forget his name, some lady with a clipboard, some man talking about group meetings in the mornings, the breakfast people . . . "

Right away, her father took charge, a resolute set to his jaw. "I'll be right back. I'm going to get you out of here. They've got you all doped up." He started toward the door.

"WAIT!" Bill's voice startled all of them. He closed his eyes for a second. "Wait," he said, softly. Something in his voice made Dana look at him carefully.

He sat up, punched the pillow into a backrest and leaned back into it, tapping his fingers together real fast, as though his insides were all still jittery like the night before.

"You don't understand, Dad. I *want* to stay. Maybe there's somebody here who can help me. PLEASE, Dad." His eyes pleaded for his father to believe him.

"*Why*, in the name of heaven, why, Bill?" Her dad's mouth twitched.

"I'm crazy, Dad. I'm the craziest person I know."

CHAPTER SIX

What does "crazy" mean, anyway? A hundred different thoughts jumped in and out of Dana's mind. Sure, she thought, if someone told me *her* brother acted like Bill, I'd think *he* was crazy. But how come if he *knows*, he doesn't stop *talking* like that?

Her mother sat on the edge of the empty bed next to Bill's staring at him in dismay. "Listen, dear, you've been under stress lately . . . moving clear across the country, new school."

Her father interrupted. "Bill, you're certainly not crazy, so stop *that* talk. Maybe, I've put a little too much pressure on you at a time when . . . well, I ought to lighten up a little. Might be a good idea for me to have a look at your courses. Maybe they've got you loaded down." Suddenly, he pointed a finger at Bill and his eyes went wide. "You haven't been experimenting with any of these damn drugs, have you? You're in trouble with me if you have."

Bill shook his head.

Dana knew he wouldn't do anything to wreck his brain. Once he told her he wondered what he'd do with all the thinking he did. "Thinking's so great," he had told her that day, pointing to his encyclopedias. "Look at all those thoughts for so many centuries."

"I can't spell anymore." Bill's voice was flat.

"What?" Dana asked.

"Some words don't spell right, like 'haven't'—it means something else. I can't figure it out. And I can't use 'won't' anymore, or 'when.' If I try to write those words, Coach Loughlin screams at me. He told me not to write words beginning with W." Bill pushed his pillow on the floor and lay flat on the bed, staring at the ceiling.

She looked hard into his face, trying to figure what he was talking about. "Maybe you misunderstood him. You could ask him what he meant."

"He's dead. Remember? He died when we were still in Boston. He talks to me out of his pictures. Even though he has the face of a dead person, he can talk to me."

Wow, that's creepy, Dana thought, stepping back. She held her breath. How could he think something so creepy?

Her father stood rigid. "I've got to talk to somebody here," he whispered, backing out of the room.

Her mother's voice cracked as she touched Bill's shoulder and said, "We'll be right back."

Dana stood alone in the room watching her brother. "What can I do, Bill?" she asked. But his eyes had turned inward as though she'd left the room, too. He might as well be nowhere, she thought. She wanted to shake him and scream, "Stop it! Stop it!" But all she could think was that her brother, Bill, was embedded alive in this other Bill, and she didn't know how to reach him. When he rolled over and faced the wall, still as a stone, she left the room to find her parents.

Near the attendants, she dropped down on the couch and burst into tears, rocking back and forth, aching from head to stomach. Tears poured into her mouth and all over her white shirt. "Oh, Mom, what's happening to him?" she cried when she felt her mother's arms around her. When the worst of the crying was over, she realized her father was talking to Rosa and Juan at the desk. "Which doctor's in charge of Bill?" His shoulders trembled.

Juan walked over to a computer. "Let's see. Bill's been assigned to Dr. Day." He turned to Rosa. "Didn't anyone tell the family?"

Rosa looked apologetic. "I thought somebody had." She searched among papers on the shelf. "Two-thirty Monday afternoon. His office is right downstairs. Here's his card."

"You mean to tell me Bill's going to lie down there all weekend before anyone even *sees* him? He's hallucinating. He's all doped up."

Rosa looked defensive. "Dr. Day *has* been seeing Bill. Several times. And I'm sure he'll call you, or you can call him."

Juan spoke up as well. "I'm a psychiatric social worker and I've been observing Bill, too. There's no emergency. If there were, there are other doctors here." He brought up Bill's chart on the computer again. "We have your phone number. Meanwhile, tests are being run, patient profile put together, evaluations made." He was polite but firm.

Rosa smiled. "Cheer up," she said, arranging twigs and handmade-looking paper flowers in an earthenware vase. "First thing Monday morning you won't know the place. The doctors will be seeing their patients. We'll have group at ten-thirty. I believe Bill feels comfortable with us."

Dana could tell by the sarcastic look on his face that her father didn't consider them "medical people." No white jackets.

All of a sudden, visitors poured in the front door to the desk, asking what rooms their daughters, fathers, or sisters were in, how they were doing, how much longer they'd have to stay.

Her father's face was ashen as he turned to Dana and her mother and said, "We might as well go home."

Dana thought her mother looked awful. Her eyes were red from crying, and her hair lay damp around the edges. Her father must finally have noticed because he put his arm around her and said, "This has surely taken its toll on you, Libby."

She nodded numbly.

"I want to say good-bye to him," Dana said.

They went down to Bill's room, but he'd fallen asleep. Her mother covered him with the edge of the spread. "I'll bring your toothbrush next time," Dana told him, and then added, because she wanted so much to comfort him, "and maybe a surprise."

When they got home, Dana helped her mother put the teakettle on and then sat at the table too confused to climb the stairs to her room. Her father went into the living room and sat with an unfolded newspaper in his lap.

Outside, a fine drizzle fell and a strong wind blew palm fronds off trees into the street. Limes blown from a neighbor's tree rolled down the driveway. This was the first rainy day Dana had seen since moving to Pasadena, and it fit her mood.

"Bill's probably having a nervous breakdown sort of thing that will go as fast as it came," her father said, walking back in the kitchen.

Her mother sat at the table, a crossword puzzle in front of her. "If only we *knew* the doctors here. Do you think it would do any good to call Dr. Edwards back home?"

"That's a good suggestion, Libby." He reached for the card file by the phone.

Trixie had run in joyous circles when they first came home, finally settling under the table. But now she stood by the back door obviously wanting to go for a walk.

"Better take her out."

Oh, Mom, I don't want to go out there, Dana thought. What if that woman is around? But Trixie scratched at the door, so Dana pulled on her raincoat and went out. She didn't turn right, toward that woman's house. Instead, she turned left to Lake Avenue, where she turned north toward the mountains, running fast and dragging Trixie behind her, until she'd gotten to where the neighbors couldn't have seen the ambulance.

She had left the house reluctantly but now with the rain on her face, she brightened. The washed leaves of the trees and bushes glistened in the clean air. The streets were lined with trees that were different from the elms, maples, and oaks of New England. For a brief time, she forgot about Bill and ran for blocks splashing in puddles with Trixie. But the mood ended abruptly as a terrifying thought whirled inside her head. She stopped as though she'd been punched in the stomach.

Am I going to get like Bill? she wondered. Two years from now will *I* be thinking crazy thoughts? After all, two years *ago*, Bill was my age and just a regular kid. She shuddered as she tried to imagine what was to become of her. What if I start talking crazy and don't know it, she thought. I'd hate to have anybody hear me. She walked slowly along unfamiliar roads, trying to bear the burden of these scary new thoughts. By the time she got back to the house, her heart was so heavy she could hardly pretend to smile.

When she walked in the door, her mother shouted, "Ian just called."

Dana walked upstairs quickly, her head bent low. "Okay. Thanks." She locked her bedroom door and lay on her bed holding a pillow over her head to muffle her crying. Crying for Bill had been bad enough, but crying for herself was worse. Every time she'd think about what might happen to her, she'd quickly change the subject in her mind because she could hardly bear her thoughts.

But you can't cry all the time, and after a while Dana got up and looked out the window at the rain. *That* made her sad, too, because she remembered herself and Bill as kids making bets to see which raindrop dripped to the bottom of the window first. She sat quietly listening to the rain, feeling lightheaded. When the redness in her eyes was gone, she washed her face and went downstairs.

Her mother looked at her closely and said, "Why don't you relax today, Dana. By the way," she added, "Dr. Edwards told Dad that Parson's Hospital has an excellent rating and he'll talk to Dr. Day. We feel a little better."

"That's good." Dana had thought Dr. Edwards was boring.

"Dr. Day called Dad again to confirm the Monday appointment and repeat the tests being done although there were no results yet."

Dana only nodded.

Her mother said, "Come on upstairs to help me change the sheets on Bill's bed."

When she walked into the room, Dana saw right away that all the oranges and peels had been cleared away. The telescope was back on the shelf above Bill's desk. But Coach Loughlin's picture still faced the wall. She felt uneasy standing in Bill's room without him. Even though she wanted to, she couldn't bring herself to turn the picture. That was Bill's picture.

She shook the pillow out of the old pillowcase and reached for the fresh one. "How's Dad doing?"

Her mother spoke over an armload of bedding. "I hope he holds together until the appointment, he's so anxious."

"I'm going down with you."

"I'm not sure that's such a good idea, Dana."

"I just have to know, Mom. Bill's my brother."

"For all we know, the doctor won't even permit you in."

"Then I'll sit in his waiting room so I can find out right away. I'm going."

When she ran downstairs to ask her father, he said, "Of course. Why not? Think you can make up the work?"

"Sure, Dad. It will only be two afternoon classes at the most. Anyhow, I'm going."

Her mother said, "I'll write you a permission slip to get out of school early."

That afternoon, Dana gave Trixie a bath in the kitchen sink then spent a long time on the floor brushing her. She wished she had a friend to talk to but she'd only lived here a month. Even her best friends back home seemed like kids she'd known such a long time ago that she didn't feel like calling or e-mailing them. Half her girlfriends had had crushes on Bill. How could she tell them he thought Coach Loughlin talked to him from pictures. They knew that coach was dead. She'd tell them when he was better.

She felt like a nerd sitting around with her parents on a Saturday afternoon instead of doing things, but she could never just call Joannie, or even Sheila, and she hardly knew any of the other girls in her classes yet. The whole neighborhood seemed to be full of old people, nobody her age. And she didn't call Ian back.

Her mother stood by her computer, leafing through "Vanity Fair" magazine. Dana knew she had planned to write articles on places in the Pasadena area like Santa Anita racetrack, Caltech and the Rose Bowl. Then, she planned to drive up to the mountains to Big Bear and Lake Arrowhead and down to the Pacific Ocean. Poor Mom. She had a thousand plans. Today she had only turned on the computer to check for e-mail messages, but Dana didn't think she'd sent any, except maybe to Aunt Deb.

Her father put on a CD of Beethoven's Ninth Symphony and sat in the living room listening—always his way of dealing with problems. All of a sudden, he jumped up, punched his hands together and roared into the kitchen. "Bill might have had a concussion from some soccer accident we hadn't known about. That makes sense to me.

That's a pretty rough game, you know. Doctors have been warning about head injuries for years." He paced the room, exhilarated by his diagnosis. "I'm putting in another call to Dr. Day to make sure head X-rays are taken." He had another idea. "When we go down tonight, I'll leave a note for him at the desk."

Her mother cheered up immediately. "Do you think that's possible, Clark?"

"Of course, of course. I'm telling you, Libby, these doctors don't know what they're doing half the time. We'll get Bill out of there. There's nothing wrong with our family."

Dana felt calm, almost silly. She realized there *could* be a simple explanation for Bill's behavior—nothing to do with her, nothing that could happen to her. I'll bet he hit his head once and it's just showing up, she told herself. Or, maybe he has like a brain tumor that could be destroyed by a lazer beam and he'd be fine the rest of his life. Her body tingled with joy.

The wind had stopped, but the rain pounding the roof sounded like music. Dana went to the front door and looked outside. The air smelled fresh and the wet grass sweet and flowery. She took a deep breath. A tiny lizard had been frightened when the door opened, and darted back and forth before disappearing under a rock. Poor little thing had scary things happen to him, too. Life poured back into Dana while she stood in the open doorway. Maybe she'd worried for nothing. She decided to phone Ian.

He sounded glad to hear her. "I was afraid you weren't going to call me at all. Is everything okay?"

She remembered what a nice voice he had. "Okay, I guess. All the test results aren't back yet so the doctor doesn't really know what's wrong. But Dad's going to have them X-ray Bill's head in case some old soccer injury is . . . making him act strange. He's pretty sure that's what it is."

"I guess it could be something like that."

She took a deep breath and asked the question she hadn't dared to think about all day. "Do Sheila and Joannie know? And Eric?"

"I don't know. I haven't talked to them. I've been developing pictures most of the day."

"I suppose with all those neighbors seeing the ambulance, and the police, they're sure to find out. Don't you think so?"

"Maybe. But you don't have to tell them anything," Ian said.

"I know, but that's what I'm like. I hate secrets. I have this dumb habit of always telling the truth, even sometimes when everyone would be better off if I didn't say anything."

Ian laughed. "Hey, I've got a couple of awesome pictures of you for the paper."

"Oh, no," she squealed, "I'll bet my ears stick out."

"Only one."

"Don't dare put my picture in the paper without *showing* me."

"Are you going to school Monday?"

"I guess so."

"I'll show them to you at lunch."

"I hope they're not nerdy."

"Only a little," Ian laughed and hung up.

Dana ran up to her room, her heart thumping with happiness, to decide what she'd wear to school. She hadn't worn her yellow pullover yet and all the silver rings, and the rope choker with the shells. That and her jeans would be fine. If anyone asked about Bill, she'd say her dad had figured out what was wrong. She stood by the window remembering how exciting it had been to dance with Eric. She could almost feel his closeness as she relived that fantastic moment. The next dance was almost a month away. Maybe she would help Sheila plan it. Just regular hip hop might be fun.

She tore off the top of a movers' carton that was full of shoes and boots and hanging canvas shelves and began organizing her closet. After that, she would open the carton with all her flowered pillows and curtains. Dana looked around her new California bedroom. It was a really nice room.

CHAPTER SEVEN

Monday was warm with bright blue skies. The rain had cleaned the air, and the mountains stood brown and clear with snow dotting the tops. You'd never see that in Boston, Dana thought, snow on mountains and rose bushes blooming at the same time. Pasadena was kind of a cool place.

As Dana waited for the school bus, Bill and his problems faded further from her mind. At breakfast her father had assured her, "You'll see. When the doctor looks at those X-rays, that will be that." Dana had felt relieved. By the time she stepped off the bus into the school yard, she had decided she'd say her dad had figured out what was wrong with Bill, if anyone asked about Friday night.

Sunday had been a long, draggy day. Bill had slept through their visit, although the woman at the desk—not Rosa, a skinny older woman named Marilyn with tobacco-stained fingers—told them Bill was doing fine. Dr. Day had said the same thing when he returned her father's phone call, promising to take a good look at Bill's X-rays. Dana felt glad to be back at school and planned to join a thousand clubs and also find out if anybody lived anywhere around Lemon Grove.

The whole morning went okay, mainly because she didn't see anyone who knew her real well. When she got to the lunch table, Ian was already squeezing the usual four packets all over a cheeseburger.

"I've decided to become a vegetarian," she told him, sitting across from him and unwrapping an avocado-and-tomato sandwich.

"I suppose I could manage it for a while, but sooner or later I'd have to have some MEAT." He grinned a silly grin at her.

She looked anxiously at him, hesitated a second, then said, "Ian, I'm kind of nervous about talking about Friday night." She realized everybody at the table would probably hear her.

Ian looked at her with his frank brown eyes and said, "I told you—you don't have to tell anybody anything."

"Suppose someone just *asks?*"

"Tell them it's not catching," he whispered.

Dana giggled. Just then, she looked up and saw Eric sauntering toward the table, his tennis racquet in one hand, a plate of spaghetti and meat balls balanced waiter-style in the other. I know he's a show-off, but he's so gorgeous, she thought, watching him flash his amazing smile around. But, still, Dana looked down at her lap as Eric sat next to Ian. If *he'd* seen Bill, how would he have reacted, she wondered.

Then, Sheila came over, her arms full of animal books. Dana thought she must have read everything in the library.

Joannie was just behind, smiling around at all the tables as though she was a finalist in a beauty contest. They sat on either side of Dana, across from Ian and Eric. In no time, to Dana's relief, everyone was talking about the dance.

"Lookin' good!" Eric told Sheila. "Those posters were terrific."

Joannie tossed her head and said, "Did anyone notice that I danced every dance?"

"What's the next theme?" Dana asked Sheila, still grateful the talk was about the dance.

"I thought it might be fun to watch people disco to 16th century Italian madrigals," Sheila teased, and tore a bag of popcorn with her teeth.

"Super night for everyone," Eric said, then looked sheepishly at Dana. "Sorry. Everything okay? At your house, I mean."

Dana caught her breath at the unexpected shift in the conversation. This was one time when she was tempted to lie. The moment she'd dreaded all weekend had come. "Fine."

He shot a quick look at Joannie, "I thought I'd heard there was some kind of trouble at your house and—hey! I didn't even know you *had* a brother."

"Well, I do. His name is Bill, and back at Paul Revere he was a pretty famous soccer player and practically a genius, and the only reason you never heard about him is because he's over in the senior annex and older than we are and . . . " Keep your voice down, Dana told herself, her heart pounding in her chest, and *don't cry*.

Joannie interrupted. "It isn't as if anybody wants to pry, Dana. *I* only want to try to help. It's just that, well, my mother met some neighbor of yours who said there was some kind of problem at your house Friday night, maybe connected with your brother."

Dana straightened her back, trying to look calm. "He was acting . . . like all wired. So Mom—she got worried—called an ambulance because Dad and I weren't home and we don't know any of the neighbors yet." She stopped to lick her lips.

"This neighbor told my mother a police car was there and an ambulance and the men practically had to put a straitjacket on your brother. And they took him away strapped to a gurney. Is that true?"

"*No*, they *didn't* have to put a big straitjacket on him. Nobody even *mentioned* one." Dana felt mad at Joannie for being so blunt.

"I'm sorry, Dana. I guess I'm asking personal questions. But you know how important I think it is to be frank. Where is he now?"

Dana wanted to say it was none of her business. "He's in the hospital and the doctor has ordered X-rays. My dad . . . they think it's a head injury from soccer."

That wasn't really a lie, but it wasn't the truth either. In a way, she felt like a traitor talking about Bill, but in another way she was glad she didn't have to keep it a secret forever . . . at least not all of it.

"That'd be great." Joannie paused for a moment, then said, "I'm sorry if I hurt your feelings, Dana. I just wanted to make sure everything was all right because . . . "

"What's he on?" asked Eric, sarcastically.

"Cool it, Eric," Ian said.

"*He's not on anything.*"

"Sorry. Sounds as though everything's okay," Eric said, absently looking around the room.

He's not listening, Dana realized, hurt. I'll bet he's looking for that cute girl he danced with Friday. She wished people would think of her as cute instead of "nice."

Then, Joannie leaned forward and asked, "Is your brother . . . ?"

All of a sudden, Sheila slammed her fist down on the table so hard her juice can jiggled. "Shut up! NOW! This is all nobody's business. She doesn't have to tell anybody anything." She smiled quickly at Dana.

"Okay, okay." Eric seemed surprised at the outburst.

Sheila turned to Ian, her face red, and in a loud voice, obviously changing the subject, said, "Do *you* have any suggestions for the next dance?"

"We could line dance to chain gang recordings," he teased, and winked at Dana.

"Hey, great," Eric hooted, spearing a meatball.

Joannie threw her eyeballs to the ceiling and said, "Well, I only want to help . . . . "

Dana was grateful to Sheila, but still surprised at the way she'd acted. Dana relaxed. She'd lived through lunch hour. She glanced out the window. A boy in shorts and rolled-up sleeves tossed a frisbee to a golden retriever out in the school yard. The sun had burned the snow off the mountains already. Dana felt happiness pour into her bones as she realized telling her friends about Friday night had been easier than she expected.

But of course she hadn't really told anyone the truth, had she?—not about Parson's or the oranges or the coach or Bill's name in the stars . . . or the crawling bugs. But there would be no reason to, after her father talked to Dr. Day about the X-rays.

She hurried from lunch to the office with her permission note to leave school early.

Dr. Day's office was downstairs in another part of the hospital. Dana was surprised to see such a large underground area with offices, a lab, conference rooms, and a pharmacy. The doctor didn't look at all like she'd expected. He didn't have a beard and piercing eyes like Sigmund Freud. Instead he was small, stooped, fair-haired and clean-shaven. And he was younger than she'd expected, maybe about thirty-five.

When her father asked if Dana could be included, the doctor said, "Absolutely. Bill has told me a lot about you, Dana." The four sat in leather chairs around a coffee table. "Help yourselves," Dr. Day said, pointing to the coffee maker and mugs on a shelf against the wall and soda cans on a table in front of them.

Dana felt confidence in the doctor from the start. She sat back in her chair excited in a strange way to be in a real psychiatrist's office. A box of tissues was on the table next to him. Probably people cry a lot, she thought.

"I'm very glad you could come." The doctor smiled at them. "Bill's a great kid."

"We're so worried about him," her mother said, and pressed her lips together. Her father slid to the edge of his chair and spoke right up. "I wonder if you have the results of the X-rays I talked to you about. I think there's a simple explanation. As I told you, Bill played soccer back in Boston. As a matter of fact, he was on the winning team for a whole season, and it occurred to me he might have a head injury we didn't know about."

Dr. Day had listened patiently and now looked at a chart on a clipboard. "Well, now, because of your concern, X-rays were taken from several angles and studied by two of our doctors." He paused. "However, nothing in them indicates a cause for his current problem . . . no sign of fracture or trauma of any kind, no swelling."

Dr. Day spoke slowly and politely. Nevertheless, Dana knew he'd shattered all their hopes. She watched her father collapse into himself and wondered, now, what she could tell everyone.

Dr. Day leaned back in his chair. He seems to be taking his time, Dana thought, waiting for us to ask questions.

"What about drugs?" her mother asked. "They're such a problem in the schools. Bill says he didn't take any, and we believe him, but you hear such awful stories."

Dana almost hoped it would be that simple, and maybe it was true. Bill had always been kind of a loner, never with the "in" or "out" group. True, he played soccer and was in the astronomy club, but most of the time he was just Bill, studying, reading, watching TV, lying on his bed thinking. *Would* he take drugs?

"All the lab tests were negative. That's the first thing we test for." He handed a sheet to her father who glanced through it then handed it to her mother. "No, Bill hasn't been taking drugs. And he's in good physical health."

"He's always been healthy," her mother said, "even as a baby."

Dr. Day looked at his clipboard again, slipping one sheet out from the packet. "You certainly knew the family history well, all the way back to the great-grandparents," he told her mother.

She smiled. "I think women pay more attention to information like that than men do."

"I agree. It looks as though most of the ancestors died either in their fifties of cancers or of heart problems in their eighties. A few with diabetes, I see. Two of the older generation had TB, diphtheria." He seemed to be talking to himself. "Pretty straightforward.... This bridge accident—was that a suicide?"

What a funny question? thought Dana.

Although she looked puzzled, her mother answered right away. "No. That was my grandfather Evers. He was walking across the bridge in Hudson Falls when a milk truck lost its brakes and hit him."

Dana could see her father stiffen.

"What's that got to do with Bill?" he asked, impatiently.

Dr. Day looked up, setting the clipboard aside. "I just want to get some background information on the family." He spoke to all of them when he asked, "When did you first become aware of a change in Bill?"

Her father didn't answer. Dana and her mother looked at each other and answered at about the same time. "Back in Boston, I guess."

Dana said, "Even in his junior year, he started coming right home after school and not staying after for anything, not even the astronomy club anymore."

Her mother said, "Dana's right. Bill has always been a quiet boy but he became, I guess the word is withdrawn, didn't even want to go out to dinner with us or to a movie." She shrugged. "I thought he was just being a teen. But ... "

Dr. Day looked up quickly.

"Well, he became funny about food, picked little things out of mashed potatoes, food like that, and put it in the garbage."

Dana slid forward in her chair. "Mom's right. He told me once that dust from the ceiling contained poisonous particles."

Her father said, "Ridiculous. Bill has always been quiet, yes, but he loved sports. He would never have quit the soccer team if he hadn't found out I was being transferred out here."

Her mother said to herself. "Hadn't he quit *before* you . . . ?"

Dana couldn't keep her thoughts straight. What *could* be wrong with Bill anyway? A part of her didn't want to know now. Even her father didn't seem about to ask the one question they all wanted the answer to.

Instead he said, "How long will he be here?"

"That's hard to say." Dr. Day got up and poured coffee into a white mug that read DAD in red letters. "A few weeks at least, perhaps a month this first time. It's important to get him stabilized on the proper medication before he goes home."

"Medication? You mean to take for a long time?" Her mom seemed appalled.

Dr. Day nodded. "The medication will quiet him, help him sort out those bewildering thoughts he's having."

"He thinks he sees his name in the stars," Dana told him.

"So he tells me."

Her father waved his hand in the air. "That's just Bill's imagination."

Dr. Day went on. "He has responded well to the medication I've put him on . . . a combination of Stelazine and Artane, two of the earlier, proven drugs. There are promising new drugs being developed all the time and a great deal of research is being done. We will also try Clozapine although regular blood testing is required. And Olanzapine. I'm very optimistic."

The room was quiet as Dana and her parents stared at one another, then at the doctor.

Dana had sat with her hands in her lap trying to sort out her own bewildering thoughts, but suddenly had to know. She found her voice and asked, "Then, what's wrong with Bill?"

The doctor leaned forward and spoke directly to her. "So far, Dana, all of the tests point to the possibility that your brother has a mental illness. We'll continue testing, evaluating, watching over him, but we think he's . . . he may be . . . schizophrenic."

CHAPTER EIGHT

"Schizophrenic?" Dana repeated. Hadn't she heard the word in health class? Hadn't they been shown a film about it? It wasn't like "epileptic" or "diabetic." What was it?

Her father jumped up and almost lunged for the doctor. "Don't be ridiculous."

"There must be a mistake," her mother said, emphatically, her face pale.

Dr. Day shook his head back and forth very slowly.

Dana gripped the arms of her chair, recalling the film in health class to which she'd only half paid attention. She shivered. There'd been a kid who had religious things going on in his head and thought he was sent by God to do something strange, and a girl who wore a robe she'd made from a blanket because she thought she was a Druid priestess. Kids in class had giggled during the film. Even she had laughed, especially at the girl because she'd had such a weird look on her face. But Bill couldn't be *that* crazy, could he?

"Is that why Bill thought the picture talked to him and bugs were all over him and people in space tried to contact him?" she asked, eyes intent on the doctor.

"That's right, Dana. Schizophrenics sometimes seem to lose their senses. They see, hear, taste, feel, and smell things in a strange way that makes them act, well, kind of odd."

Her mother's voice cracked as she said, "You read such awful things in the paper . . . that people like that . . . sometimes . . . there is *no way* Bill . . . "

"Very, very few . . . make the newspaper," the doctor quickly assured her, "especially when you consider that this is a disease that afflicts one to two percent of the population."

Her father had been sitting slumped over, listening, but now interrupted. "That means there are two to three million in this country. Could that be right?"

"That's right." Dr. Day went on. "Some are barely troubled by the symptoms and function quite well. Others . . . others seem to get a bigger dose of it and have a harder struggle." He smiled at Dana. "We'll try to make Bill's life as comfortable as we can."

Still, Dana's face was grim. "Did he catch it? How did he get it? What *causes* it?"

"Nobody is really sure, but there are definite structural changes in the brains of people with the disease." He looked right at Dana. "Sometimes it's genetic."

"What does that mean?" she asked, leaning forward.

"That means it runs in families. It has to do with genes. When it is genetic, then in about half the cases someone else had it . . . mother, father, brother, sister, grandparent, aunt, uncle . . . which leaves the other half . . . "

"There's never been anything like that in either family as far back as I know about," her father told Dr. Day. "You saw that family chart Libby put together . . . never anything like this."

"All the things I've worried about with the children, I never, never worried about this. Never." Her mother was deep in thought. "No. Nobody that I can think of . . . "

Her father asked, "What were you going to say about the other half?"

Her mother listened intently when Dr. Day said, "It had been known for a long time that a higher number of schizophrenics were born in the late winter or early spring in the northern hemisphere during the 1950s. That triggered research in several parts of the world . . . from Scandinavia to right here in California."

Her mother said, "My goodness. Bill was born January 30th."

"Yes, I noted that. Well, new research points to a virus mothers may contract during the middle trimester of pregnancy when the infant brain is developing."

Dana knew he meant the three middle months.

Her mother half whispered. "Clark, remember how sick I was

that October we went to Canada when I was pregnant with Bill . . . ?"

Her father reached for her mother's hand and nodded.

"There are probably many different causes of this disease. Just recently, research out of the Netherlands points to a famine during the Second World War that caused a high incident of schizophrenia among babies born to women pregnant at the time."

Dr. Day looked right at Dana and she realized he was telling her as much as he could and still being optimistic. "Believe it or not," he went on, "in some rare cases it is a deficiency of one of the B vitamins, niacin. The symptoms of pellagra are very much like schizophrenia but nowadays it is seen in only the very poorest, most undeveloped areas."

"How long is he going to be like this?" Dana asked.

"Some people have one episode and never have another. And a very small percentage require long-term hospitalization, but I don't think that Bill . . . " He hesitated, looking from face to face. "Others are plagued with it all their lives, to one degree or another, and eventually do better in what are now called residential care facilities where they are with people who understand them and know how to help them deal with the disorder."

Dana pictured that film again. People in one of those places sat on couches and chairs watching television as if they didn't care what they were looking at.

Her mother gasped. "Call them whatever you want, they're just plain old board and care homes. We would never put Bill in one of them. Never."

"You probably won't have to given Bill's level temperament. As a matter of fact, the majority of schizophrenics are cared for in their own homes. They are withdrawn, quiet, stay to themselves, but function quite well on the proper medication."

Dana sat stunned and silent. Other questions tumbled around in her brain, but she wanted to go home and think about what she'd already heard. She glanced at her father but he was slumped forward, his elbows on his knees, his head bowed. Her mother, too, seemed lost in her own sad thoughts.

Dr. Day said, "I realize it's hard to take this in all at once, but I am glad you were together when I told you. As I said, we are still doing evaluations, studying test results, so let's hope for the best." He glanced at his watch. "And keep in mind that this disorder is the focus of *tremendous* research right now. We're very close to finding not just the causes, but a cure." He put the clipboard aside as if the session were over. "When you think of how quickly people dying in diabetic comas recovered when insulin was first discovered . . . one injection and while you looked at them they got well enough to go home in a few days . . . it could happen here as well." He stood and looked directly at Dana. "Please, call me whenever you have questions, Dana. Bill is lucky to have such a supportive sister."

She was about to stand when her father spoke in a low voice. "Doctor, please, I have a question. He doesn't, well, Bill doesn't hear voices, does he?" There was perspiration on his forehead.

There was a pause. "Sometimes." Dr. Day sat back down. Dana remembered that film again, and shuddered. Did Bill hear voices like those kids had? She asked, "Whose voices? What do they say? Can he see their faces? Does he hear his own thoughts out loud or something?" Her eyes pleaded with Dr. Day for an explanation.

"It's thought the frontal part of the brain is affected by the disorder and that . . . "

Dana jumped as her father's voice exploded in her ear. "*What you're trying to tell us is that Bill is insane!*"

Dana saw Dr. Day's expression soften as he leaned toward her father. "Mr. McAllister, I never use that term. Bill has a brain disease that will some day be curable. Meantime, we can help him deal with it."

When they got home, Dana felt she should close the drapes because the bright, sunny day didn't match her feelings. She stood in the kitchen doorway not wanting to be with her parents but not wanting to be alone either.

Her mother sat in the rocker, absently rubbing her forehead.

"I don't know where to begin to understand what has happened." Tears came to her eyes.

"I won't accept it," her father said, rolling up the sleeves of his white shirt. He had put in a call to Dr. Edwards and now nervously paced the kitchen.

Dana thought, what does "schizophrenic" mean, anyway? Then she remembered her computer. Trixie was right behind her as she ran up the stairs to her bedroom. As soon as she typed in www.schizophrenia.com, a million different selections came on the screen. Starting with definition, she read: "Schizophrenia (dementia praecox)—a mental disorder in which the person withdraws from reality into a mental world of his own." That sure describes Bill, she thought. Then, she read a long section that scared her more than Dr. Day had. It said that the people became more and more confused, or what is called "psychotic," until they sometimes have to be put in a mental institution *forever* to protect them from themselves and society. What was worse, it said society sometimes had to be protected from *them*.

What terrible thing is happening to us? Dana wondered, her eyes skipping along the frightening lines. She could hardly finish reading the article, it scared her so much. It also said the condition usually appears in the teens in men, but in the twenties in women, which made her worry about herself again.

"I just know I'm going to get it," she told Trixie. The little spaniel put her paw on Dana's shoe and wagged her tail.

Dana sat at her desk concentrating on each thought to see if it made sense. But what good did that do? Bill's crazy thoughts made sense to *him*.

Then, all of a sudden, a new thought formed in her head. What if Bill had accidentally been given a drug once, like that LSD she'd read about, and he didn't know it—some mean joke by some creep in school. Something in his soda. What if that had happened a long time ago and was only showing up now? She'd heard about delayed reactions. Probably wouldn't show up in tests this late. Things like this happened.

Dana sat up straight to think about this. Sure. That's probably what happened. So there's no reason for me to worry. I don't even have any of the symptoms Bill has. She clicked the mouse on where she had seen the list of symptoms and read: delusions, hallucinations, disorganized speech, loss of will.

"I know I never heard voices trying to control me," she told Trixie. "And I've never seen things that weren't there." She felt so much better. She didn't think she could have stood the pain of reading that section much longer. It was too medical. Later, she would read some of the other articles.

Feeling almost cheered, she went back to the kitchen. Her father was finishing a conversation with Dr. Edwards, and had collapsed into a chair. "He spoke to Dr. Day and seems to think the diagnosis is correct. He's asked for the report, but he said the symptoms are pretty classic." He put his head in his hands. "What a terrible thing, Libby," he said softly.

Her mother put an arm across his shoulder. "What did he say when you asked why he'd never noticed anything wrong with Bill?"

"He said schizo . . . he said this disorder is difficult to diagnose in children. It rarely shows up until the late teens, early twenties. No one knows why." He shook his head. "No one seems to know anything."

"We've got to find out what we're dealing with, Clark. I'll go to the library tomorrow." She pointed to her computer. "I'm sure I can find something here but, right now, I've had about as much information as I can handle."

Her father nodded in agreement, his eyes closed.

Dana didn't mention the web site she'd found. She hoped her mother would find more optimistic stuff to read, more up-to-date information about the new medications and research. And she didn't say anything about her idea about the mysterious drug. She wanted to believe it so badly she was afraid they'd have a reason why it couldn't be true.

After dinner, the three drove down for the evening visiting hours.

Ruth was at her desk again and before buzzing them through the door, she beckoned them into her office.

"Here's a brochure about the National Alliance for the Mentally Ill. You may want to join. As you can see, there are chapters in all fifty states so this is not a rare disorder your son has." She smiled comfortingly. "Find a coping group near your home. It helps to talk about problems with people who share them." When her mother thanked her, Ruth added, "Take care."

They found Bill in the lounge, sitting on a chair in the corner, idly turning the pages of a *Sports Illustrated* magazine. Dana touched him lightly on the arm and handed him a pack of gum. "Here's your present."

"Thanks." Bill stood and gave her a little laugh as he put the pack in his pocket.

"Trixie's fine," she said, pulling a chair close to his.

"Oh, good."

"How are you doing?" Her father shook Bill's hand, a forced smile on his face. He pulled over two more chairs.

"Okay."

Dana noticed that Bill was still wearing the same shirt he'd had on on Friday and it kind of smelled, so she was glad to see her mother hand him a fresh shirt, underwear, and socks.

"Thanks," Bill said. "They make us shower and everything."

Dana glanced furtively around the cheerful room with its yellow walls, green plaid upholstered couches, and colorful posters. An upright piano stood in the corner with a platter of cheese and crackers on top. A teenage boy with ink drawings of dragons and monsters all over his arms and face played Ping-Pong with a middle-aged man in a bathrobe. Dana looked through the window to the enclosed court where the same teenage girl she had seen the first night sat at a picnic table, not moving, just staring down.

Dana looked back when her mother asked, "How are the meals?"

"Okay, I guess."

"What was for lunch?"

Bill seemed to have trouble with the question. "I think it was chili. The staff served it because they'd lost a bet on some game and . . . " Suddenly, he looked up as though he saw something moving slowly across the ceiling, then slumped forward, his head in his hands, as if whatever he saw had confused him.

Aren't we going to tell him we saw Dr. Day? Dana wondered. Are we just going to talk about food and the weather?

Dana watched her mother pull fuzz off her tweed skirt and heard her father clear his throat and then not say anything.

Dana looked around the room again. Over on the couch sat a man about forty talking to a motherly looking woman. The woman asked him if he'd watched "Jeopardy."

The man shook his head, his hands over his ears.

The woman laughed. "Most of the time I can answer the questions but I'm not fast enough." She was knitting something blue.

"I tried to watch," he lowered his voice to a whisper, "but a dog keeps barking in my head." His hands flew back to his ears.

Dana's skin prickled when she heard that, but the woman went right on knitting. "That won't bother you so much, once the new medication is regulated."

Dana looked back when her father said, "We had a talk with Dr. Day this morning, Bill, and—"

"Please, Dad, I *know* what's wrong with me. I went to the library a long time ago and looked it up."

Dana thought she'd never seen such a bewildered and hurt look on her father's face. "Why?"

"Because . . . I kept hearing a voice saying 'blue shoe,' 'blue shoe' over and over all day long."

Her mother said, "That doesn't make sense."

Bill didn't comment. "It went on for a couple of days. The minute I woke up it started." He hung his head. "It scared me."

Her father shook his head. "Why didn't you tell me?"

"I just though I could handle it myself, but . . . I kept shorting out." He sighed. "Then, it stopped. Years, really. I think I was only about thirteen then."

"I should have been told."

"You'd have said I was crazy." Bill laughed sarcastically.

"Couldn't you have told your mother?"

"I didn't want to scare her."

Her mother looked deep into Bill's eyes and said, "You've carried this burden a long time, haven't you?"

Bill nodded. "But, it went away . . . for a long time."

Her father said, "I'm sorry, Bill. We're going to get to the root of this. I promise you. You'll be yourself again in no time. These doctors don't know everything."

"The medication certainly seems to have helped you." Her mother smiled a cheerful smile.

She's right, thought Dana, he does seem calmer, and he's making sense. But when she looked at him, she saw she was wrong.

The comment had set off something, because a dark look came over Bill's face. "I don't like the medication. It takes away my feelings. One of my brains has died." He jumped up and paced around and around their chairs, circling behind them. "You keep asking about meals, Mom. They're putting something in them. Today the smell was awful—even plain milk tasted like vinegar." Then, he whispered to Dana, "It's only safe to eat food in cases."

"Food in cases?" she repeated, her eyes wide.

"Yes, oranges or hard-boiled eggs. Even apples aren't safe because the skin is so thin something could easily be injected into them. I think that's why I slept all day Sunday. They didn't want me to know what happened." He glanced at the door as though someone had just looked in. "Listen, Mom, you don't know what they're out there doing to people's brains. You're easy to fool. You'd believe anything."

Her mother only gazed at him, her arms hanging.

"Half of them have badges they don't have to show you."

Dana was pretty sure that being suspicious of people was what paranoia meant. Bill was acting paranoid. She looked from her mother to her father and back at Bill. Nobody said anything. Nobody cried. She could hardly remember what her brother used to be like. She tried to picture him half-walking, half-running onto the stage in the school auditorium back home the night he received the National Merit Scholar award, his green eyes sparkling, his expression so bright. He was proud of himself, and her father had bragged to everyone in the world about his brilliant son.

Afterwards, when the four of them had gone for pizza, Bill had talked about how great he thought astronomy was and that all he wanted for his birthday was a telescope. Dana could hardly keep from crying as she remembered the night she looked through that same telescope trying to find Bill's name in the stars.

CHAPTER NINE

Over the next three weeks, Dana gradually became accustomed to having Bill in Parson's. She didn't visit him every evening if she had a lot of homework or if she stayed after school with the yearbook club to help pick out snapshots for the "after school" pages. Some nights when she did go down, she was really bored. Most of the time Bill was lost in his strange thoughts anyway.

The Bill who used to be was becoming a memory, and this new Bill, down at Parson's, didn't quite fit into the family somehow. Whenever she passed his room without the usual clutter, it looked more like a guest room. After a while, Dana felt like Sheila—like an only child. She joined the girls' tennis team and stayed Tuesdays and Thursdays for lessons. Sometimes she'd catch a glimpse of Eric on the boys court serving the ball with his tan, muscular arms. Once in a while, if she caught his eye, he'd nod and ask, "How's it going?" She knew *he* didn't have a crush on *her*. Still, she couldn't shake the way she felt about him. Every time she saw him flash that amazing smile, she felt weightless.

Sometimes she'd visit with the kids watching the cheerleaders practice, and cheer when Joannie did something particularly sensational with her baton. Or she'd talk with Ian while he walked around, always alert to snap a picture for his "California Characters" collection. She thought of joining the girl's track team herself. She'd been a good runner at Paul Revere.

Dana felt happy at Wilson High. It was her favorite place to be. Joannie was right, fun *was* fun. And life at home became more peaceful as the weeks passed. There were just the three of them now, although she noticed her mother sometimes forgot and set the table for four.

She hardly thought of Bill some days, so she had mixed feelings when her father told her, "Bill is being discharged Saturday."

Her mother had said, "That's wonderful news, isn't it, Dana? Thursday is Thanksgiving. We'll have a quiet dinner right here." She began making out a grocery list, writing down the things she'd need—poultry seasoning, cranberry sauce, olives, pumpkin.

Dana had stiffened briefly when she heard the news. She'd forgotten how to talk "regular" with Bill. But right away she felt happy that they'd be a family again and that Bill could sleep in his own room. Later, she put the new *National Geographics* magazine that had come for him on his desk with the others.

The morning they brought Bill home, Dana and her parents met first in the doctor's office. "He's pretty well stabilized on the medication," Dr. Day told them. "Let's see how he does at home."

"How often does he need to take it?" her mother asked.

The doctor went over the different prescriptions with them. "Bill can handle that. He's not disoriented. He knows exactly what he's supposed to take and when. The nurses have gone over it with him."

"Does he *want* to come home?" Dana asked. Bill didn't seem to care about anything, not even Trixie.

Her father must have had similar feelings because he added, "He seems so remote when I talk to him."

"Schizophrenics *are* remote—withdrawn. It's one of the symptoms, and they often react to situations in kind of a flat way. And then, too, the medication has a dulling effect. Schizophrenics on medication rarely do anything of importance. But, yes, I think he's looking forward to going home." He glanced at his clipboard. "I've set up an appointment for three o'clock the Tuesday after Thanksgiving."

Her mother said, "I'm so nervous. There's no danger he'll be as . . . confused as he was the night we brought him here, is there?"

Dr. Day shook his head. "As long as he takes his medication, barring an unusual or upsetting incident he'll be able to keep those," he hesitated a second, "distractions on the back burner."

"When can he go back to school?" Dana asked.

"I doubt for the remainder of this term. As for next term, we'll have to wait and see."

Her father leapt from his chair. "You mean he'll miss a whole term? What good is the medication then?"

"The medication, I must emphasize, is not a cure. Whoever finds *that* will get the Nobel Prize. The medication helps him tell the difference between what he's hearing and what he's really thinking." He looked at his clipboard again. "Bill is on one of the thorazine derivatives. That is the major tranquilizer developed in the sixties that made it possible for so many of the mentally ill to leave hospitals and go home, or at least to less restrictive facilities in their own communities. This medication works particularly well on schizophrenics."

Dana saw her mother wince. "That word is so hard to hear. Dear God, will I ever get used to this?"

"Are you telling us that if it weren't for these drugs Bill would have to live in a mental institution?" her father asked.

"Perhaps, some of the time."

A chill ran across Dana's back. She decided to ask him a question that had bothered her ever since she'd talked to the lady on her block. "Bill couldn't get dangerous, could he?"

"Unfortunately, Dana, you're going to find that a great many people equate bizarre behavior with dangerous behavior. And, of course, it *does* happen once in a while that a mental patient feels threatened or cornered for some reason and lashes out. Naturally, in those cases it's best to leave the care of them to trained professionals. But, in truth, schizophrenics have a crime rate far below that of 'sane' people."

"Bill's not dangerous," said her father, emphatically.

"I agree." The doctor tapped a pencil on his finger. "We can only go by past behavior, but I've seen nothing to indicate he's anything but an intelligent, thoughtful boy to whom a pretty devastating thing has happened."

"He wouldn't . . . he hasn't thought about suicide, has he?" her mother asked.

"He looks so sad," Dana added.

"There are unfortunate statistics that show that the suicide rate is high among schizophrenics. The burden of the symptoms is sometimes awfully hard to bear, but Bill seems stable to me."

Her father said, "I see now why you asked if Libby's grandfather Evers' death had been a suicide."

Dana saw tears start in her mother's eyes. "I've always been a little afraid of the mentally ill, avoided them. But when it's someone who was once your baby . . . " Her father nodded and lowered his head.

"In addition to the symptoms of the disorder, each has his individual personality." Dr. Day leaned forward in his chair and spoke directly to Dana. "In all the years I've treated them, I've found the mentally ill to be the most frightened, the gentlest, the bravest people I know."

When Bill walked into the kitchen, Trixie was so glad to see him she ran round and round the table, knocking over her water dish.

"I had trouble remembering her," Bill said softly. He sat in the kitchen rocker with the little dog in his lap.

"Well, Bill," her father said, walking stiffly back and forth, "it's good to have you home."

"I'm glad to be home," Bill answered, scratching Trixie's throat. Then, he pointed to the computer in the corner. "How's the writing going, Mom?"

"I've started a piece on the Hollywood Bowl." She darted around the kitchen, nervously fixing lunch, watching Bill out of the corner of her eye. "I'll have this salad made in just half a second, Bill, and I've *smothered* it in your favorite avocado dressing. It's just for you— that and piping-hot biscuits."

Her father pointed toward the den. "I thought we could watch the football game. The Redskins are . . . "

Bill jumped out of the chair. "NO! No. The people talking at me are . . . . No. Maybe later."

Hardly anyone spoke during lunch, unless one of them asked Bill a dumb question like "Haven't the mountains been lovely lately?" or "Isn't it good we had some rain?"

"Big change from Thanksgiving weather in Massachusetts, hey, Bill?" her father asked, his voice too loud. "The temperature here today was in the eighties."

Bill looked as though the idea was too complicated to understand.

After lunch, Bill went to his room and lay down. Dana thought it was almost a relief not to have to talk to him and then felt rotten for feeling that way. The whole day was like that. He'd stay in his room for a while, come down and stand in the living room staring out the window, and then sit in the kitchen rocker with Trixie in his lap.

Sunday was the same except Bill slept almost sixteen hours, plus taking a nap. "Dr. Day said the medication would make him drowsy," her mother explained. "I thought it might perk him up to walk Trixie, but he keeps putting it off. I don't want to nag him. I don't know how he feels, so I've been doing it, or Dana."

Her father said, "I thought he and I could drive over and rent a few videos, but he said maybe some other time, so I didn't press it."

Her mother looked bewildered. "Something about the images seems to bother him."

Late Sunday evening, as Dana passed Bill's room, she poked her head in and asked, "Want a bowl of chocolate chip ice cream?"

He'd been lying on his bed, his hands folded under his head. "Sure, thanks." He sat up, pulling his pillow into a backrest.

When she returned with it, a sudden rush of affection made her sit on the edge of his chair and ask, "How do you feel, Bill?"

"Oh, I don't know, Dane, different for sure—kind of as if I'm supposed to fly apart, but I won't—and kind of as if I'm in some kind of danger, but I don't think I am." His forehead creased as he concentrated on her question. "I feel blunted. The electricity is gone from my brain."

"Maybe the medicine's making you feel that way."

"I think so." He lifted the spoon halfway to his mouth then said, "Dane, I know I'm a failure but . . . "

"No!"

"But I feel I'm meant to do almost extraordinary things. Maybe I'll write or paint or invent something fantastic." He put the dish down and went over to look out his window. He waved his arms, his green eyes bright as he gazed at the sky.

Oh, no, thought Dana, he can't still be thinking his name is up there. "Maybe you'll be an astronomer after all, Bill."

"Maybe. It's funny, but it's still all in there." He pointed to his head. "I still remember everything I ever learned. Trouble is, I don't seem able . . . " He handed Dana the bowl of half-finished ice cream. "Thanks, but this doesn't taste like regular chocolate chip."

Wilson High was open all day Monday and Tuesday but closed at noon Wednesday for the start of the Thanksgiving holiday. Dana was glad to be back just for those few days. School had become a refuge for her, a place to escape the problems at home, a place to have fun. She didn't tell anyone Bill was out of the hospital. Nobody asked except Ian who passed her Wednesday as she headed for the bus. "Say, how's Bill doing?"

"Well, the doctor discharged him. He's home."

"Great. What's he doing?"

"He mostly just hangs around and sleeps a lot."

Thanksgiving Day her mother cooked a turkey big enough to feed twenty people. From early in the morning, the house smelled like stuffing, sweet potatoes, and apple pie. Dishes of nuts and candies were everywhere. The dining room table was set with the good bone china and blue linen tablecloth and napkins, and just before they sat down, her mother lit tall, yellow candles.

Bill seemed to enjoy the meal, although he didn't have a whole lot to say except "This is great, Mom" two or three times. Dana found herself peeking at him sideways. It was not knowing what he was thinking that made her uncomfortable. But then she decided you never know what *anybody* is thinking, even someone sitting right next to you that you've known for a thousand years. She glanced at her mother drinking cranberry juice and her father reaching for the mashed potatoes. She didn't know what they were thinking either, but then she wasn't worried that they were thinking crazy thoughts.

Her father stood at the table carving the enormous Thanksgiving turkey. He carved it with the old bone-handled carving set that had belonged to his father, and before that his grandfather. On special occasions, he used to tell Bill that the honor of carving would be his someday. But that day he didn't.

By Friday, Bill started to talk more, stayed in the living room or kitchen with the rest of the family. He brought his *Sports Illustrated*s down to the living room. From time to time he'd laugh at something he'd flip past on one of the pages. The time passed slowly for Dana. She still wished she had friends like she had in Boston. They'd do things together outside school, like go to the mall or a movie or sleep over at each other's houses. But she didn't know anyone here that well yet, and there still didn't seem to be anyone in her neighborhood even near her age. She passed the time reading or straightening her room or walking Trixie, but the long, boring four day weekend dragged on.

Saturday evening Bill surprised her by poking his head into the den where she sat reading and asking, "How about a game of chess?" in a voice that had lost its flat tone. Dana decided it probably took a while to adjust to being home after being in a hospital for so long. Now he was beginning to act like himself.

"Sure. I'll beat you, too." She closed her book and ran to the closet for the chessboard.

"Yeah, right," he chided, setting up the board with the little wooden pieces he'd carved out of balsa wood when he was a cub scout.

Bill threw himself into the game and tapped his left foot up and down very fast the whole time he played. His eyes looked bright as he concentrated on each move.

Dana thought the game was going fine but looked up quickly when Bill said, "I don't know what the knight wants to do."

Oh, no, she thought, stiffening. She wanted to say something, but she was afraid she'd embarrass him. He had been such a good chess player. Now he sat hunched over the board talking as though the chess piece were a real knight. Finally, he dropped his hand on the board, and with an almost frightened expression, said, "I can't figure anything out."

"Don't worry about it, Bill. We can play some other time."

"*What's the matter with me?*" He jumped up and the board and little wooden pieces flew all over. "Damn it, Dane. *What's going on?*" He kicked the board across the room.

She backed away. "Please, Bill."

"Do you know what you're looking at? The biggest freak in town." He turned and ran out of the den and upstairs.

All day Sunday Dana felt nervous about the way Bill was acting. Late in the day, she heard her parents talking in the den about whether they should call Dr. Day.

"Are you sure he's taking his pills?" her father asked.

"He says he is. He showed me the bottles and it looked as if he'd been taking them the way he is supposed to. Dr. Day made it clear I wasn't to pry. Bill is an adult and the nurse at Parson's spent a lot of time teaching him the names of the medications, what they do, what the doses are, the side effects." She rubbed her temples. "I've got the worst headache, Clark."

"I'm sure you do." He kissed her forehead. "I guess we can manage until Tuesday. It would even be hard to describe how he's acting. We'll have to get used to this, but I don't know how we're supposed to know how to deal with it."

Her mother shook her head. "Without any training . . . just turned loose to deal with a mental disorder that baffles experts."

Dana couldn't wait to get to school the next day. At least she'd be with normal people. What good's a four-day weekend if you don't want to be home, anyway?

CHAPTER TEN

Monday morning Dana woke before her alarm went off. She dressed in white shirt, jeans, and Guatemalan vest, sprayed a mist of "Apple Girl" scent on her hair and clothes, and was at the bus stop fifteen minutes early. The ivy was still beaded with dew, and snails inched their way toward its cover before the sun came up. She was so anxious to get back to school she was even thinking of reasons to stay after. Maybe she'd do some homework in the library and catch the late bus, or practice her tennis even though the team didn't meet on Mondays. The back of her neck felt chilly in the early morning air and oddly stiff as well. Then, she realized she'd been holding it tense whenever she talked to Bill. She looked across the road at her house. The branches of the pink camellia hung gracefully by the living room windows. The pomegranate tree in the side yard was heavy with red, leathery-looking fruit. Her gaze went up to Bill's window. Dr. Day will have to put him back into the hospital when he sees how he's acting, she thought.

Hopping off the school bus that crisp November morning, Dana was smiling. She went from class to class feeling freed from the heaviness at home, and put the long, gloomy weekend in the back of her mind, almost giddy with relief that it was over. At lunch, she didn't even tell anyone Bill was home. After all, no one asked about him anymore anyway. She wanted to keep the happy feeling all day. Even Mrs. Pelotte's class wasn't too boring.

When school let out that afternoon, she hung around in front for a while, reluctant to get on the bus. The burden of trying to figure how to act with Bill brought the stiffness back to her neck. Then she felt guilty again. Poor Bill. He couldn't have had much fun that day. Maybe he'd be glad to see her. She sighed. Well, she'd just talk to Sheila for a minute and then leave. Sheila stood over by the bike racks, so Dana headed in that direction. Ian was up ahead, his camera slung over his shoulder, as usual. When she got closer to Sheila, she saw Eric standing, bent forward with a puzzled look on his face. She followed his gaze to the path through the trees leading from the street to the front of the school. What was he looking at? Suddenly, the whole place fell silent. She turned again in the direction Eric looked. She was aware that Ian had his camera focused in the same direction. But at what?

Click.

Now she saw . . .

Click.

Oh, no! Oh, please God, NO. Her whole body sank. Bill was coming toward the school in his "Commonwealth of Massachusetts" T-shirt but only his undershorts. The shorts had tiny blue polka dots and strings hung frizzy from the waistband. He had some kind of dumb rag wrapped around his head, and was passing out oranges.

Click.

Don't scream, she told herself. Things began to blur. She backed away in horror then stopped and thought, How can I get him home? She started toward him but stopped when he said, "They're safe. They're in cases." His eyes had a wild gleam to them as he peered from face to face.

Kids looked at one another, puzzled.

Joannie was over to the right making a face as if she had eaten a worm.

"How safe are bananas?" one kid shouted.

Dana heard sniggers here and there. She wanted to run to Bill, but stood frozen.

"*He's* bananas," shouted Eric. Dana heard the sarcasm and hated Eric, and yet . . . Go home, please; go home, please; oh, Bill, PLEASE go home, she pleaded, silently.

"What's your web site? crazy.dot.nut?" some kid hollered.

Dana continued to stare at Bill, his long bare legs white and thin as he shivered in the chilly November air. Then, she lowered her head and didn't speak.

"Hey, who *is* that?"

"The guy's crazy," someone else yelled.

"So are you. Why don't you shut up?" It was Sheila, shoving some boy Dana didn't recognize. Sheila and Joannie were now just in front of her. She didn't talk to them.

Mr. McCarty, the principal, came out and went up to one of the teachers.

"I've called PMRT," he told her, his voice low.

The teacher nodded, not taking her eyes off Bill.

"What's that?" some kid nearby asked.

"People trained to deal with . . . situations like this. They'll know what to do." The principal went down into the crowd. "Everything's all right. Why don't you all just go about your business." He started toward Bill but stopped just outside his range. Bill took a step back and peered suspiciously at the principal through narrowed eyelids.

"This is *embarrassing*," Joannie said. "Doesn't he know what he looks like? Why does anybody let someone like that walk around. I was supposed to meet the cheerleaders—now I'll be late."

Sheila hung her head, one hand covering her eyes.

Eric shouted, "Somebody snare him in the nut net," then grinned around at the kids who laughed.

Dana knew that once she might have laughed, but now . . .

A couple of kids moved in Bill's direction and he quickly reached up to hold the rag on his head, dropping his bag of oranges as he did.

"Help me," he pleaded, stooping to pick them up.

A lot of kids went over and helped him pick up his oranges, some just laughed nervously, most stood frozen.

Bill held the rag on his head with both hands, pulling it across his mouth and tight against his ears. Dana was sure he was hearing those stupid voices.

Sirens wailed in the distance, coming closer and closer. Soon, an ambulance pulled up as close as it could and two men in T-shirts, jeans and running shoes ran up the walk. Dana could see they weren't Victor and Artie. When Bill saw them, he panicked and tried to run through the crowd, accidentally knocking down a girl, scattering her books. He tripped, cutting a gash in his bony white knee. When some kids tried to hold him, he lashed out at them, struggling to get free, screaming, "Help me! Help me! My bones hurt."

An orange rolled close to Dana, but she didn't pick it up. She kept stepping back . . . away from the orange. Nobody paid any attention to her. Everybody was watching Bill, except Ian, who now had his camera turned toward *her*.

Click.

She was hardly aware of him. She felt dizzy. She watched, almost screaming, as the two men did their best to subdue Bill, finally coaxing him into the ambulance. "Come on, kid," one of them said, "you're going to be okay."

Bill kept yelling "Help!" but Dana didn't help him. She turned and ran across the school yard, and all the way up the street. She had an awful pain in her side and her heart pounded against her ribs. Still she ran, her mouth full of tears. Even when she couldn't run anymore, she kept running. When she burst into the kitchen, she collapsed into a chair gasping for breath. Her mother was on the phone.

"Clark, hold on. Dana's just run in and—oh, God!—something's happened. She's hysterical. Dana, is it Bill?"

"Crazy," she gasped. "He's so crazy."

"Clark, come home right away. Please."

Her mother ran a washcloth under cold water and held it to Dana's forehead. Soon the pounding stopped and the pain in her side faded. She pushed her mother's hand away, took a deep breath, and shouted, "*I hate him. I hate him.* He's wrecking everything."

"I'm so sorry . . . I thought he was in his room . . . I went down to do the wash . . . when I checked . . . he was *gone*." She turned in circles in the middle of the kitchen floor, trying to explain.

"Why can't I have a normal brother like other girls? I wish he'd—I don't know what—disappear or something. I *hate him*."

"Dana, believe me, I understand. I don't know how we're going to live through this." She started to cry herself, wiping her eyes on a tissue. "Where is Bill now?" She sat next to Dana.

Dana felt her mother's arms around her as she told her, between sobs, what had happened.

Her mother jumped to her feet. "Where are my keys? We've got to find him."

Then her father's car roared into the driveway and screeched to a stop. When he rushed in and heard the story he said, "We've got to find out where they've taken him." His face was gray and desperate-looking. "What in heck kind of medication has that doctor got him on? For all we know it's *causing* the problem."

Her mother grabbed her purse and started toward the door. "Let's hurry," she said.

Her father beckoned for Dana to follow.

"*I'm not going with you,*" she screamed, her heart pounding like a hammer in her chest.

"Why?" he asked, then closed his mouth and said no more.

Her mother poured a glass of ice water and put it on the table in front of her. "Dana, I'm afraid to leave you in this state, but we've got to find where they've taken him."

"I hope you *never* find him." But she knew most of the anger had gone out of her, and waved for them to go without her. She sat with her head bowed as sobs shook her thin body.

After her parents left, Dana continued to sit at the kitchen table, alone, confused and brokenhearted, trying to figure what to do. Maybe she could move back home, live with Aunt Deb, finish school there and never come to California again. She just wanted to stay in the house for the rest of her life. She longed to be in her soft bed with warm covers over her head, but she didn't have the energy to move.

Suddenly, Trixie began barking at the back door.

It was Ian. Dana was surprised to see him, but so glad.

He burst into the room when she opened the door. "That was Bill, wasn't it? I didn't recognize him at first with the cloth on his head."

She nodded.

"Wow!"

They sat across from each other at the kitchen table.

"What happened? I thought he was on some kind of medicine and lying around all the time." He unzipped the top of his blue parka.

"I don't know." She wiped at her swollen eyes and nose with a tissue. "I can't go to school tomorrow. How can I tell everybody that was my brother? You don't know what he used to be like. I was always so proud of him. Half my girlfriends had crushes on him, always wanting to go to soccer matches with me to see him. Now look. He'll never have a girlfriend his whole life."

"He *was* pretty weird."

"And something else is bothering me, too," Dana admitted. "I feel so ashamed of myself." She covered her face with her hands.

"Why?"

"Well, because . . . " She stopped and hung her head, remembering how frightened Bill had looked, shivering in the cold air, his shirt hanging half off him, his white chest looking all pinched. "When Bill dropped his oranges and said 'Help me,' I ran home." She turned her face away.

"Hey, listen, Dana, don't feel guilty."

"Kids who didn't even know him picked up his oranges for him." She looked down at her lap. "Besides, all the way home I wished Bill would . . . go away someplace . . . forever."

"I think anybody would feel that way."

"I wished they'd have to lock him in one of those facilities where he couldn't get out."

Ian thought about that. "Might be hard to lock up a kid forever for passing out oranges in his underwear."

Dana put her face in her hands and wept.

"Hey, don't cry. Face it. His *reason* for passing out the oranges almost makes you want to back off."

Talking to Ian made her feel a little better. She took a deep breath and tried to think clearly. "The doctor told us it's a disease. That's so hard to believe. I don't know why he can't just talk Bill out of his crazy thoughts."

"I suppose it if were that easy, he'd have done it."

"Oh, Ian, I don't know what to do. I only just moved here. Nobody knows me, and nobody knows Bill. Wait, I'll show you a picture of him taken . . . PICTURE!" Dana jumped to her feet and ran to the other side of the kitchen away from Ian. "I remember now! You took a picture of Bill—for what? your 'California Characters'? for the school paper?" Her hands shook.

Ian ran over to her, but she pushed him away. "I didn't know it was Bill. It's a habit. It's what I do. I take pictures."

"And you took *my* picture, too!" she screamed. *Where is your camera?*"

"It's locked in my locker at school." He grabbed her wrists. "Calm down, Dana."

"I want those negatives," she sobbed.

"Hey, those are *my* pictures."

"You're worse than Eric. At least with him you know what to expect." She ran to the kitchen door, flinging it open. "Get them!"

Ian left, turning once but Dana had locked the door.

Dana was asleep at the kitchen table when her parents came in later that night. She raised her head and sleepily watched her mother collapse in the rocking chair. She looks as though she has hardly any bones in her body, Dana thought.

"Where's Bill?" she asked, looking from one to the other.

"Back in Parson's Hospital," her father told her, leaning against the kitchen counter.

"What happened to him? Why did he act worse?"

"He'd stopped taking the medication." Her mother snapped open a can of iced tea from the fridge.

"Why?" Dana yawned, nearly awake now. The scene with Ian suddenly burst to the front of her mind. I can't tell them about those pictures, she thought. Not now.

"All sorts of reasons. He didn't like the way it made his brain feel. He thought the doctor was poisoning him. He thought he could handle it himself." She sighed. "Dear God, he's *so* sick."

"Well, won't *you* have to give him the pills now?" That made sense to Dana.

Her father said, "Dr. Day says Bill must understand how important it is that he take the medication. He's learned a lesson now. Apparently what he did is not uncommon. So, he'll be in the hospital for a while, and—"

Her mother interrupted. "By the way, Clark, you'd better read that insurance policy. It's very confusing and I'm not sure this stay will be covered since he's being readmitted sooner than one month after discharge, or some such wording as that."

"Good Lord, Libby. It better cover him. I got the best insurance policy the company offered."

"Well, it's hard to tell just how much it covers mental illness. It seems to treat it differently from other diseases. I get the feeling they wish they didn't have to cover it at all because it costs them money."

"Between the doctor and the hospital we could be bankrupt in no time. Not that I'd *care* if I thought it would make Bill well, but I can't even seem to get *that* kind of assurance."

Dana saw how tired her parents were and felt selfish for caring so much about herself, but the image of Bill in those dumb shorts, with the dumb rag on his head wouldn't leave her, and her shame and guilt and worries about herself were too painful to handle anymore. She had to know what else the doctor had said.

"Does Dr. Day think Bill will be better when he comes home the next time?"

"Who knows?" her father said. "It's like running through a field putting out brush fires."

Her mother said, "He thinks Bill understands what . . . "

Dana saw the three of them for the rest of Bill's life trying to figure out what he was saying, what he was thinking, where he was going. What he was wearing! *It wasn't fair*. "But Dad, Bill is so *crazy*. Why doesn't the doctor think he should stay in the hospital forever until he's better?" Her stomach muscles tightened.

"It's the law. Believe it or not, Bill's not sick enough to be hospitalized permanently. He's not suicidal and he's not planning to hurt someone else."

Her mother added, "There's a legal term called "gr̥ disabled" which means the patient is unable to take care of things like food or clothes or a place to live . . . like the homeless people who are mentally ill. But, of course, we would always take care of Bill."

"Then that means he could show up at school any time he wanted, doesn't it? *Doesn't it?*" Dana jumped up and started out of the room.

"Now wait, Dana," her father said, blocking her way. "Don't think your mother and I aren't aware of what this is doing to you."

Her mother reached across the kitchen table in Dana's direction, but she looked too tired to stand. "Somehow or other we're going to see this through."

"See it through? What's that supposed to mean? It's like some awful monster thing has come into the house." Dana felt her mouth quiver and covered it with her hand. She was about to push past her father when she saw, for the first time, that the veins on his temples stood out and a deep V creased his forehead. He looks old, she thought, alarmed. And Mom's right eyelid twitches all the time now.

Dana's throat pinched tight as the thought came to her that her parents might not be able to protect her the way they always had—not even from her own brother—and panic ran through her body.

"*You don't understand!*" she screamed. "What if he stops taking the medication again? How come it's all up to *him*?" She knew she was going to cry but wanted to ask the one question that worried her the most. "*What if he comes to school* NAKED?"

CHAPTER ELEVEN

Dana walked as slowly as she could along the noisy hallway toward the lunchroom. She was late but wanted to make sure everybody was at the table so she wouldn't have to tell her miserable story twice. For in her heart, Dana knew she would have to tell her friends that day. They were sure to find out and would hate her for not telling them first.

The memory of Bill handing out oranges in his underwear popped in and out of her mind as though someone kept poking a snapshot in front of her eyes. How could he do such a thing? She stopped briefly, pretending to search for something in the pages of her algebra book, then sighed, smoothed her hair over her ears, and went on. At the lunchroom door the mixed smells of hamburgers, pizza, french fries and enchiladas made her stomach flip. Dana'd only brought an apple to eat, and after she took one bite she immediately felt full. Before she left that morning, her mother had said, "You'll think of the right thing to say when the time comes." Those words came back now to give her courage, and feeling she might be able to blurt out her story *that minute*, she hurried toward the table, noting that everyone was there, except Ian. He's probably getting Bill's picture ready for his portfolio, she thought, or he'll put mine on the front page of the paper with the caption, "The Girl with the Crazy Brother." Hurt made her close her eyes.

She took a deep breath and sat next to Joannie who was poking a straw in her apple juice container. Sheila was sitting next to her but talking to kids in her science class about some TV program on cloning sheep. Eric was squeezing a packet of mustard on a ham and cheese and talking to kids at the other end of the table. Dana pushed up the sleeves of her white pullover and looked around.

For a moment, it seemed like any other day, but she had no sooner settled down than she heard Eric say, "Get out of here with your oranges."

"*What?*" she asked, about to scream, then saw some nerdy kid passing out oranges, rolling his eyes and tossing his head, imitating Bill.

"Dollar apiece," he said, "guaranteed safe."

Dana's heart thumped, anything she'd planned to say gone from her mind. It was as though she'd been hit by a wave and was being pulled by an undertow. She nibbled at the apple, hoping nobody would notice her misery.

"Hey, wait, give me one. I've got polka dot shorts," Eric yelled, grabbing one of the oranges.

"You're jiggling the whole table," Joannie told Eric, holding her juice container. "You nearly spilled this all over my shirt."

Sheila yelled over at him, "Come on, Eric! You're out of first grade. Remember?"

Dana gave her a grateful smile.

Eric sneered. "Come on, Sheila. This kid's *funny.*"

Some other kid grabbed a couple of oranges and ran down the aisle, juggling them.

Dana sat frozen.

Pretty soon, Mr. Chung, the gym teacher who was cafeteria patrol for the week, saw what was going on and sent the kid with the oranges out of the room. "Settle down." He strode the length of the aisle, looking slowly from right to left. "Everything's cool. Finish your lunch."

Joannie tossed her hair. "Wasn't yesterday embarrassing? I wonder where they took that weird kid."

"Who needs him?" said Eric, a grim expression on his face. "There are too many crazies already. My dad says they should lock them all up and throw away the key."

Sparks went through Dana. Apple taste came up in her mouth, but she swallowed it down. "*That's mean.* That's really, *mean*, Eric. The truth is . . . well, the truth is . . . that was my brother. He can't help the way he is. If you'd known him before this, you'd have liked him. *And, he'd never have said something that mean!*" She was shouting. Heads turned toward her but she didn't care. The whole school could know. And she wouldn't cry.

Eric's jaw dropped. His face turned red. He darted away from the table and stood by the soft-drink machine, fumbling with coins, glancing over his shoulder at Dana. When he returned with a root beer he hung his head while he opened it, then he said, "Come on, Dana, give me a break. How am I supposed to know that?" They stared at each other, and Eric looked away first. "I mean, I'm sorry and all."

Dana looked hard at Eric and thought, how could I ever have felt the way I did about him? He's just a big conceited show-off. Still, remembering the brief dance with him, she wondered if she would ever have that particular feeling again for anyone else her whole life. Looking at him with clearer eyes, she felt a lonesomeness for that feeling as it slipped down her arms, out of her body, and was gone.

"What's going on with your brother anyway?" Joannie asked, making her mouth a tiny O.

Dana hesitated a moment then told herself if she just kept talking and answering everybody's questions, sooner or later the day would be over and she could go home and collapse. "The doctor says he's . . . well, he's mentally ill." She lowered her head and whispered. "He's what's called schizophrenic."

"Wow! I've read about that," Eric said. "There was this guy who thought the electricity in his body freaked out power plants. That means your brother's *really* crazy and . . . " He clamped his mouth shut and looked away.

Dana made a tight fist and shouted, "*I know that! but he doesn't think he freaks out power plants!*"

"What's the matter with you, Eric?" Sheila hollered, punching his shoulder.

"How long's he going to be like that?" Joannie asked.

Dana wished she could say a week to ten days, like the flu, but instead said what Dr. Day had said, "Nobody knows. Maybe a short time, and maybe not. Maybe forever." She paused. "Sure, I'd rather have a normal brother." She stopped, finally feeling embarrassed. "Maybe he'll never be normal." She sniffed. There *was* a hush in the room. The whole world must have heard me, Dana thought. She stared at her lap, trying to catch her breath. Had she acted all right? Or not? Was it over?

Joannie looked back at Dana and said, "Gosh, I guess your neighbor told my mother the truth after all. But anyhow, this must be awful. Can't your parents find a place for him somewhere? I mean, he can't live at home, can he?"

"My parents are doing the best they can taking care of him."

"Where is he now?" Joannie asked.

"He's back in Parson's Hospital. The doctor is going to change his medication. Besides, he may never do anything like that again." She sighed. "But I guess we don't even know that." She pushed the apple away from her.

"How long will he be in that hospital?" Eric asked, almost politely, Dana thought.

"Maybe a couple of weeks. I'll probably go down tonight to see him."

Eric's eyes widened. "You mean you've been in that *mental* hospital?"

Joannie leaned closer. "What's it like?" She put down her egg salad sandwich. "Weren't you scared?"

Dana saw that other kids were listening, too.

"No, it's not really scary. At least not where Bill is. Of course, there's a place where the dangerous people are or the ones who tried to commit suicide. But I heard there weren't very many over in that section compared to the regular part where Bill is."

"Are there bars on the windows?" asked Joannie.

Dana tried to remember. "I don't think so. I can only picture curtains and, I think, shades. Maybe the windows don't open, like in some hotels and offices."

"Well, you can't have patients escaping," Eric said, digging a fork into a piece of cherry pie.

"To tell you the truth, Eric, the ones I saw didn't act as though they wanted to escape." She leaned back in her chair, thinking of the people in Parson's Hospital. They belonged to her new, other life. "They mostly seemed sad and mixed up, lying on their beds or going for a million tests hoping someone can make them feel better."

Suddenly, Sheila jumped out of her chair. "I'm late for the library," she mumbled, turning her face away as she grabbed her books and ran from the room.

Eric's mouth hung open. "Now what did I say?"

Dana watched Sheila leave and felt that one of the first friends she'd made at Wilson High had abandoned her. First Ian, now Sheila. Were Joannie and Eric going to do the same? She looked at Joannie.

"Oh, Sheila's always doing strange things."

"You're telling me?" Eric said, rubbing his shoulder.

The din and clamor in the lunchroom went on, but at Dana's table the group was quiet for a moment. Throughout the lunch, she had glanced from time to time at the doorway, looking for Ian. She did so again now, but Ian was nowhere in sight. Dana returned to her dismal thoughts, while Joannie peeked at her reflection in a hand mirror. Dana was about to leave when Eric put down his fork, leaned over and said, "Hey, listen, Dana. How was I supposed to know crazy meant something real?"

"That's okay, Eric. I didn't know it either."

That afternoon about four the doorbell rang. When Dana opened the door, she was surprised to see Sheila. "Hi. Come on in." She wouldn't mention the scene at the lunch table.

"I've been riding my bike and thought I'd see if you were home."

Dana introduced Sheila to her mother, and then took her upstairs to her bedroom. She looked at Sheila's big green sweater with holes in the elbows and wondered again why she didn't care about her looks.

"Oh, what a gorgeous room," Sheila said. "I love the flowered wallpaper. Maybe I can get some ideas for *my* room. Everything's plaid and it's boring." She wandered around looking at different things. But when she came to the picture of Dana and Bill at Moosehead Lake, she suddenly slumped on the edge of the bed.

"Sheila, what's wrong?" Dana sat next to her, surprised to see tears in her eyes.

"I thought you were really brave to tell everyone about your brother." She swallowed and looked at her lap.

"Now at least people know."

Dana expected Sheila to say more, but instead she went back to looking at the picture.

"You've written Moosehead Lake across the bottom. Where is it?" She held the picture up close to her face, her back to Dana.

"Way up in Maine."

Sheila took the picture to the window, peering at it carefully in sunlight. "Must be awfully cold to swim up there."

Dana smiled. "Well, people from New England are more used to cold weather and cold lakes and snow and things than people from California." She watched Sheila dust off the frame with the edge of her sweater and put the picture back on the dresser.

She half turned to Dana and said, "I'd better get home." First, she started for the door, but then went over to the rocking chair, picking up one of the flowered pillows. "I really do just love your room, Dana. It's so flowery and cheerful and . . . " She tossed the pillow back in the pile.

"Thanks." Dana wondered why Sheila was acting so . . . she didn't know what it was . . . embarrassed or something. She watched her start for the door again, then suddenly plop herself down on the chair hugging a bunch of pillows to herself. "I wish I could be as brave as you are."

"What?"

She looked so miserable, tears streaming down her cheeks, that Dana didn't say anything else.

Finally, drying her eyes on the sleeve of her sweater, Sheila started talking really fast. "I have a sister. She's younger. She's eleven. Her name is Barbara."

"I thought you were an only child."

"I might as well be."

Dana just sat ready to listen.

"She lives in Los Angeles." Sheila sighed.

Dana nodded.

"We visit her on holidays and weekends and things."

"How come nobody mentions her?"

"I never told anybody about her. Now, I wish I had . . . the way you did . . . about your brother." Sheila went back to the window, tracing her finger around the pane of glass. "When we moved here four years ago from Chicago, right away my parents put her in the place where she lives." Her voice was low. "It's called Jack and Jill Guest Home. Isn't that dumb? It sounds as if everyone in there was nursery-rhyme cute."

Dana went over to her. "What's wrong with her?"

"Lots of things. She can't read or write or understand things I tell her."

"Is she retarded?"

"Worse. She's fat and her eyes have funny lids and her face is flat or something." Sheila shook her head. "She's got what's called Down syndrome."

"I've seen people like that."

"It has to do with something called a chromosome. They all look kind of alike."

Dana agreed. "Especially the eyes."

"My grandfather said people like Barbara used to be called Mongolian idiots." Sheila covered her face. "Isn't that terrible?"

"You don't have to talk about it."

"Now I want to. I feel better." She sat on the bed, holding a pillow to her cheek and took a deep breath. "On Barbara's last birthday I got mad at my mom for not having her home for a cake. I had the stupid idea if she was away from that place she might be okay."

Dana sat in the chair across from Sheila. "What happened?"

"Mom got Barbara a new dress and brought her home. But it didn't work. How could it? Barbara's going to be like that forever."

"I'm really sorry."

"The thing is, she's gross. She doesn't even care if her nose is running."

Dana only nodded.

Sheila's expression was thoughtful when she added, "When I was a little girl, I pretended Barbara was *my* baby. I rocked her and fed her. I really loved her. But then when I got older I used to get embarrassed because people stared at her. Once, in a store, she wet her pants all over the place. She was almost seven. I wanted to die."

"I would have been embarrassed, too."

Sheila sighed. "I wish I had a *real* sister, but I know I never will." She jumped to her feet, her expression solemn. "I overheard my mom say it wasn't worth the risk to have another baby."

Dana wasn't sure how to answer.

Sheila had a pleading look on her face. "Can I ask you something?"

"Sure."

"Do you worry about heredity?"

"I know that what Bill has runs in families. I worry I'll get like him even though I don't *think* I have crazy thoughts."

Sheila said, "I know I won't get like Barbara. You have to be born that way. But I worry that if I got married, I might have a baby like her."

Dana stiffened. "I never thought of that."

"So I've decided never to get married."

"That's sad."

"I mean it. I've gotten used to the idea. I'll have an interesting career, lots of friends, and I'll keep busy helping people."

"But suppose someone falls in love with you?"

"Who'd fall in love with me looking like a bag lady?" She pulled at her messy hair.

Dana finally knew why Sheila always looked so raggy. "But, you're pretty. You can't let what's wrong with your sister ruin *your* life." She realized she was talking about herself, too.

"You're just trying to cheer me up, Dana."

"No. Don't forget I've got the same kind of problem you have." Dana looked out the window. "Sheila, it will be years before we get married. By that time there might be injections so girls like your sister could be born normal. Scientists are always doing things with genes and stuff. They cure all kinds of things now."

"How could anything cure your brother's crazy thinking? It isn't like curing a sore throat."

"I read that it is, except that the disease is in the brain and not somewhere else in the body like the lungs or heart." She smiled. "Dr. Day thinks some scientist is going to find a cure."

Dana and Sheila stood side by side, each thinking her own thoughts. Finally, Sheila said, "Maybe someday we could go to the library after school and read up on stuff—do things like that."

"Sure," Dana was really glad Sheila had stopped by. "Maybe go to the bookstores in the mall."

That night Dana dreamed the evening news was interrupted by a special report telling the world that scientists had found a cure for schizophrenia. And in her dream Dana saw Bill float above the house and on into the night sky, his telescope held high above his head as he moved among the stars.

CHAPTER TWELVE

About six that evening, Dana and her parents were sitting around the kitchen waiting for a pizza to heat through when her mother suddenly went over to her computer table and took out a disk.

"What are you doing, Libby?" her father asked, lowering the newspaper he had been flipping through.

"I'm going to format this disk." She slipped it in the B drive and punched some keys.

"Are you going to write tonight?" Dana put a container of Parmesan cheese on the table.

Her mother said, "I may only get started. An idea has been darting in and out of my mind for a while." She leaned back, listening to the computer click through the formatting process. In a quiet voice, she said, "I've written so many frivolous articles and stories over the years, but now . . . ever since Bill got sick . . . "

"What do you mean?" Dana turned her chair toward her mother.

"I've read so much lately about mental illness, particularly schizophrenia, but I haven't found anything written from the point of view of a brother or sister. You've had a lot to deal with, Dana . . . and alone. I wish I had a book to give you that would help you get through this, but there doesn't seem to be one in the libraries. Not for your age."

"So you're going to write one, aren't you?" Dana beamed, proudly.

"Yes. I'm going to try. I see so many families down at Parson's. . . . " She dropped her hands into her lap. "Maybe I can write a story that will be helpful to people like them . . . and us."

"That's a great idea, Libby."

Her mother pointed to her computer. "There is so much

information available here." She pushed "eject" and the formatted disk whined out.

Dana and her father looked over her shoulder.

"Watch! If I put in www.nami.org it will bring up the National Alliance for the Mentally Ill, that group Ruth gave us the pamphlets on. That website tells you where the AMI chapters are in all the states, where there are conferences, book reviews . . . "

Her father peered at the screen. "There seem to be pages of articles on the latest research, a help-line, and . . . "

Dana said, "There are probably lots of kids with brothers and sisters like Bill." And like Sheila's sister, too, she thought, wondering if there were a website that could help Sheila.

Dana told them about the website she had found—www.schizophrenia.com. "I know there's more stuff on that, too, than I found the first time."

Her mother said, "I'm excited about my book. Maybe you can help me with the dialogue, Dana. You could . . . "

The phone rang, startling them. They all dashed for it, but her father caught it first. His face dropped as he listened. "Yes. Yes. I'm his father. *Where is he?*"

"What's happened?" Dana and her mother asked together.

Her father cupped his hand over his ear and waved for them to be quiet. "Damn it! You mean he's *gone?*"

Dana tried to hear the person on the other end.

Her father looked furious as he continued to listen. "I don't believe this. Sure! *Sure!* I'll come down and I'll drive around looking for him, but who in hell knows what direction he took off in." He slammed the phone down and leaned against the wall, both fists clenched.

"What?" Dana asked.

"Bill's missing—has been for as long as two hours."

"How?" Her mother asked.

"Let me collect my thoughts, Libby." He took a deep breath. "It seems a patient in the locked ward smashed a picture and attacked the nurses with a shard of glass. Some of the regular staff from Ward A went to help, and that's when Bill must have slipped out."

"Maybe not," Dana suggested, staring at the phone. "The hospital is so big he could be hiding."

"They've checked everywhere."

"Where could he go?" Dana wondered. "He doesn't even have any money."

"He borrowed change from another patient, said he needed to make phone calls, so he had bus fare to who-knows-where." Her father rubbed his forehead. "And he took an orange with him."

Dana was certain he was headed for school. She didn't want to ask but had to know, "Was he still in his underwear?"

"No. Someone had found him jeans and things."

"Had he been given medication?" Her mother looked hopeful.

Her father closed his eyes and shook his head. "No, unfortunately, Dr. Day wanted the old medication completely out of his system before he tried him on a different one . . . Risperidone, or something." He paused. "The police are searching, but we'd better look for him ourselves."

"I'll get my purse," her mother told him, quickly turning the computer off.

"I'll come, too," Dana said, starting for the door.

Her father thought for a minute. "No, you'd better wait here in case we get a call—maybe even from Bill."

"I've got the cell phone," her mother added, holding it up.

"I guess it makes sense for me to stay here," Dana agreed. After they left, she took the pizza from the oven to cool, loaded a few cups and glasses in the dishwasher, then settled in the rocker to wait. Trixie slept at her feet. The house was so quiet she nearly flew apart when the phone rang. It was Ian.

"Dana?"

"Yes," she said, coolly.

"I'd like to come over for a minute."

"What for?" She hated herself for being so glad to hear his voice.

"I'd like to talk to you about . . . well . . . yesterday and show you something. Okay?"

She hesitated, wanting to ask if he had the negatives, but instead said, "I suppose so . . . for just a minute, but . . . " She told him about Bill's disappearance. "I have to stay by the phone."

"Well, maybe I'd better come anyway. What if you need to go get him? I've got a car."

"Okay."

When Dana opened the kitchen door for Ian, she stepped back stiffly to let him in. She noticed he didn't have his camera. She'd changed quickly into a fresh T-shirt, washed her face, and smoothed her hair over her ears. But now she was prepared to stand up to him. She wanted those negatives.

"Hi." Ian stood awkwardly by the counter. Trixie sniffed at his shoes, wagging her tail.

"Hi." Dana leaned against the fridge, her arms folded.

"I guess you haven't heard anything new about Bill."

She shook her head.

Trixie settled down by the rocker.

Ian leaned against the counter and said, "About the picture—first of all, Dana, I couldn't get my camera last night because the custodians had already locked the school and there was nobody around."

"Okay." She'd accept that much.

"Then, there was no time between classes for me to do anything."

"You couldn't have pulled the film from the camera and gotten the negatives for me?" Her mouth pinched tight.

"No. There were other pictures on the roll that I wanted—from the dance—from the soccer game. I'd have destroyed them if I'd pulled the film out."

"Okay." She'd accept that much, too. "But couldn't you have *told* me that?"

"I looked for you after lunch but you weren't there. I thought maybe you'd decided to skip school after . . . Anyway, I only had my lunch hour to develop the film."

"So?" He *is* polite and all, she thought.

"So, Dana, I wanted to explain something. Could we at least sit down?"

She nodded.

He sat at the kitchen table, pushed up the sleeves of his black sweat shirt with the WHS letters in red and took a deep breath. Dana sat across from him on the edge of a chair. "First of all," he told her, "I didn't know that was Bill. Right?"

"You just thought it was a great picture for your 'California Characters' book," she said, sarcastically.

"Well, sure. Face it, Dana, that's exactly what I *did* think."

And she'd give him that, too, remembering how Bill looked. "Well, why won't you give me the negatives now?"

"Let me finish. This is important." He stared at her thoughtfully. "I'm a photographer. Someday, I'd like to be a really *good* one. And I always think of the pictures I take as *mine*."

She slapped the table, scattering sugar crystals around.

"Please, Dana, wait. When you said you wanted the negative of Bill all I could think was—that's between Bill and me. If Bill gives me his permission to put it in my collection, that's all I need."

Dana listened cautiously, and said, "You mean you got permission from the injured football player lying on the field *crying*?"

"Sure. Even the lady slumped over in the wheelchair giving her cat a ride told me to use that picture. She said something about people not staying down in the dumps—whatever that means."

"But, Bill—"

"That's it. Bill really *can't* give his permission. There's no way of knowing whether he'd understand what he was giving, and so it wouldn't be fair to put his picture in my collection." He reached into his pocket. "Here's the negative. I didn't even develop it."

"Thank you. Really, Ian, thank you." She smiled and put it into her pocket. "But . . . what about the picture of me?"

"I developed it."

"You *didn't*."

"Yes. Here."

Dana looked hard at the picture Ian handed her. She saw herself, her arms extended upward toward where Bill had stood, a look of pity and tenderness on her face. She *had* wanted to help. She hadn't *really* hated him. She held the picture to her cheek and sniffed back tears. "This means a lot to me, Ian."

"I thought it would. You can have the negative of that, too. But I made a copy, for myself." He put his hand over hers. "Okay?"

"Okay." She smiled a grateful smile.

He fished around in his camera bag for the negative. "What's going on with Bill, anyway?"

She told him what she knew. "He must have just walked out of the place . . . like a visitor."

Ian opened his mouth to say something, then closed it.

"You were going to ask what he was wearing, weren't you?" She tried not to smile.

"Well, yeah, and did he have oranges with him?"

"They had found him clothes and they think he had an orange." For a second she almost felt like laughing, then the whole picture jumped before her eyes again and she thought of something. "Still." She hesitated. "There's something else about all this, Ian."

He looked across at her, his eyes keen.

"Something creepy."

He signaled for her to go on.

"Something I haven't told anybody else."

He nodded.

She bit at her lower lip then said, "It's that Bill . . . well . . . It's that he *hears voices*! I don't mean people talking in another room, or the TV. They're in his head. They talk to him all the time. Crazy talk."

He nodded. "Yeah, I've read that."

"You mean you knew?"

"I knew that schizophrenics heard voices. I just wasn't sure whose voice and why the people couldn't stop it." He gazed at the ceiling, thinking. " . . . or what the voice was saying."

"That's the creepy part." Dana shivered. "Bill told me he keeps hearing a voice telling him he's a failure."

"Whose voice is it?"

"He doesn't know. But I think it's awful that it's a mean voice."

They were sitting at the kitchen table thinking about the problem when the phone rang. Dana nearly jumped out of her chair. It was Bill. At first, she didn't recognize his voice.

"Dane." He was whispering. "Get Dad."

"He's not here. He and Mom are out looking for you. Where are you?"

"I can't get out of the phone booth."

"Why?"

Ian's face was close to Dana's as he strained to hear.

"They're pressing against it."

"Who?"

She heard him whispering, but he didn't answer her.

"Bill, where are you?"

"Where's paper and pencil?" asked Ian.

Dana pointed to the junk drawer. "*Bill, where are you?*" she shouted.

"Ask him what number he's calling from," said Ian.

"Dane, where's Dad?"

"He's not here. Bill, what's the number on the phone?"

Silence. She fought back a scream.

Ian stood next to her, pencil held over yellow pad.

"It's faded."

"Read it to me." She turned the phone so Ian could hear.

Bill's voice was shaky as he read off the numbers. "The first three numbers all look like threes or eights. Then, it looks like . . . a two maybe. Dane, I can't read the rest."

"Try!" Dana waved a clenched fist at the telephone.

Bill laughed—a loud, hysterical, wild laugh. Dana didn't ask what was funny. She knew better. It was the voices. "Dane. The walls are coming in on me. The phone booth is sinking in the sand. They're trying to dissolve my bones." He was silent, then, "Dane, please come get me. I'll wait here on the floor of the phone booth."

"Let me try," said Ian and took the phone. "Bill, it's Ian. Tell me what you see outside. Can you see street signs, stores, anything?"

The phone went dead.

Dana collapsed against Ian's chest and felt his arms around her. "Why didn't I think of that? Now, how are we ever going to find him?"

They dropped back into their chairs.

"Oh, Ian, I feel so sorry for him, hiding in the bottom of a phone booth waiting for me. What should we do? Did he give us any clues at all?"

"Could you hear any sounds?" Ian thought. "I couldn't."

"Just cars going by in the distance, making kind of a rhythmic sound. And I really concentrated on that because I knew it might be important."

"Didn't sound like he was on a main street. I couldn't hear cars braking for lights or horns honking."

"I don't think he was." Dana absently shredded a paper napkin. She was so anxious to find Bill she felt like roaring down the block to look for him but didn't even know what direction to go off in.

Then Ian said, "You don't suppose people *were* pushing on the phone booth—geeky kids or something?"

Dana shook her head. "He sounded too out of it. He said the booth was falling over. *They* were trying to dissolve his bones." She stared out the window, remembering Bill's words. "Wait, Ian, that's not what he said. He said the booth was sinking in the *sand*."

"He's on the beach." Ian paced the floor, tapping his forehead.

"And, Ian, those weren't cars we heard at all. The sound was too regular. I think they were *waves*."

"I'll bet we find him," Ian said, optimistically. "He's on the beach for sure."

"Only *what* beach? California is a long, skinny state on the ocean."

Ian sat hunched over, thinking. "I wish we could figure what to do about the telephone numbers."

"The first three numbers were threes or eights and the rest he couldn't read at all. We can't solve that puzzle. There aren't enough clues."

"Threes and eights," Ian said under his breath, then dashed for the phone book. "Maybe we can look up combinations of threes and eights and find one on the beach."

"Great idea," said Dana, leaning close to him as she felt his arm across her shoulder. "I think there's a page near the front." Wait, Bill, wait, and we'll find you, she thought, as Ian opened the thick book.

"Here's 838—Santa Ana."

"Not on the ocean."

Together, they poured over the page. Finally, Ian gave a shout, "888—Santa Monica."

"Of course, he probably took a bus to the pier."

"Let's go!" said Ian, grabbing Dana's hand.

Two seconds later they were in Ian's car headed for the Santa Monica Freeway. Thirty minutes later they drove onto the Pacific Coast Highway, parked in the nearest lot and ran quickly onto the beach. No Bill.

They stared ahead at the famous wooden structure jutting into the Pacific Ocean, lit by the full moon. Dana said, "I don't think he could be *on* the Santa Monica pier. You can't hide in the bottom of a phone booth, laughing hysterically, without someone noticing."

They headed there anyway.

Clusters of people strolled along the pier, or fished, or just hung over the railing gazing at the moonlit waters. No way could Bill be there, and there was no phone booth in the sand.

They ran back down to the beach.

"Maybe somebody already found him, maybe he's back in the hospital, maybe he took a bus somewhere else." Dana hung her head, discouraged. She peered up and down the peaceful beach. Only a few people here and there were sitting on blankets or walking along the shore. Some were running dogs. Then, she noticed a phone booth at the far end of the parking lot.

Ian nodded and they ran toward it. It was empty.

"We're not going to find him," Dana said.

"Maybe there's another one," said Ian, looking around.

"Maybe I'd better get Mom and Dad on the cell phone in case

they know something . . . tell them where we are." Just as she was about to step into the booth, Ian said, "What's that?" and picked up a piece of cardboard.

"That looks like Bill's writing," Dana said. "He probably wrote it with the pencil dangling from that string."

By the dim ceiling light in the phone booth they read:

> I'm all alone
> I can't figure anything out
> My bones are dissolving
> Bill is being destroyed
> The ocean heals

They ran at once toward the ocean. The moon shone brightly on the water so they could see out a great distance. Dana would have run into the waves if Ian hadn't held her back. "*Bill! Bill!*" she screamed.

"*Bill?*" Ian's deep voice echoed far out on the water.

Silence, except for the waves.

"Bill. It's me, Dane. Oh, *please*, come back," she sobbed.

The shimmering, moonlit top of the water created a hundred bobbing heads, a hundred floating Bills. Hysterical, Dana ran farther into the cold waters, drenching her shoes and jeans, shouting Bill's name over and over. Ian's arms held her back. Finally, she turned sobbing against his chest. Bill was dead. His body would wash up on the beach in a day or two all bloated and horrible, and for all the rest of her life she would never be able to tell him she loved him.

Dana turned and stared out across the ocean. "Bill's life was so terrible lately. If he really meant to drown himself, maybe I don't blame him, Ian. I know that's an awful thing to say, but now maybe his poor mind will be peaceful—not tortured and frightened. Oh, but I wish he hadn't done it. He may have gotten better. And what if somebody finds a cure?"

Ian put his arm around her waist, led her back to shore, and said, "I don't think he understood what he was doing. That note was so mixed up. He thought his bones were dissolving and the ocean would heal them." He looked down at Dana. "You know, I never even knew him."

"He was just a regular kid who was supposed to grow up to be a nice person—only this terrible thing happened to him. It's not fair." She dropped to the sand, discouraged. "What should we do?" She gazed along the bleak shore.

Ian still stood, scanning the water. "*Bill.*" he shouted, and then again, "*Bill.*" Nothing. He dropped down next to Dana and took her hand. "I give up."

Dana sat silent, her head swaying to the rhythm of the waves lapping against the shore. She felt numb and discouraged. Slender rivulets of water crept toward her, filling depressions in the sand. She stared at them, dreamily, then screamed, pointing. "*Footprints!*"

"Where?" Ian asked. Then he saw them as well.

Dana ran, half stumbling, following their direction. Could they be Bill's? "There's another. See?"

Ian was next to her as they followed the prints. Suddenly, Dana stopped, pointing toward a figure in the distance lying face down. "Bill," she whispered and ran toward him. It seemed to take forever to run through the dense, wet sand. "*Bill,*" she called when she got to him, but he didn't move. She saw that he was drenched with ocean water.

Ian said, "He's lying awfully still, maybe . . . "

But Dana bent to touch him, and he cried out, pulling away from her. She stood back. "Bill, it's Dana and Ian." She gasped, as he slowly turned over and she saw the look of fright, confusion, and exhaustion on his face.

"Dane? My bones . . . "

She knelt next to him. "It'll be all right, Bill." There, she said it again.

Bill's voice was husky. "The ocean didn't help. I can't walk."

Ian said, "I'll bring the car up to this parking lot. Hang on, Bill. I'll be right back." He handed Dana his cell phone. "Do you want to call your parents and tell them we've found him?"

She nodded and watched him run off.

Her father answered on the first ring and gave a shout of relief when she told him. Her mother was right there next to him, listening. Dana could tell from the crackling on the phone that they were in the car but they were able to understand everything she told them.

"Can Ian drive him to Parson's Hospital?" her father asked. "Dr. Day says Bill will have to be readmitted, and this time, he's urging us to consider having him live in a facility where he can be supervised." He paused. "We think we'd better."

"Just for a short time," her mother added, "until he's able to think better and takes his medication."

Her father's voice was solemn. "Dana, do you think he was trying to drown himself?"

"No, not really." She read him the note again. "We think he thought the ocean would heal his bones."

"Dear God," her mother said. "He'll be safer with people who understand this awful thing . . . "

Her father said, "Your mother is right. If he had drowned, we might never have known the reason."

Dana told them Ian would drive them to Parson's, that she'd meet them there. "I'm going back to Bill."

Bill lay on the wet sand, his hands folded under his head, his eyes slowly, sadly scanning the sky. A million stars twinkled in the black night. "Look at that, Dane. It's so incredible. What are they all for?" He closed his eyes and rolled away from her.

Dana walked to the ocean's edge and stood alone by the dark shore, fighting unhappiness back. She knew she could never be really happy again—not the way she'd wanted to be when she moved to California, not the way Joannie wanted to be happy. But with the hope that Bill could find some peace with his life until a cure was found, she supposed she could be happy enough.

When she saw Ian's car drive into the parking lot, she ran to meet him. A sudden rush of emotion that went beyond gratitude filled her heart, a feeling far deeper than any she had ever felt for Eric.

Together they helped Bill walk up the beach to the car and drove him to Parson's Hospital.

AFTER GRADUATION

Bill McAllister—after his delusional attempt to cure his dissolving bones in the ocean, Bill was declared "a danger to himself" and readmitted to Parson's Hospital. As Dr. Day pointed out, his irrational act might have had the same consequences as an attempted suicide—his death. He was discharged after a one-month stay, and, at Dr. Day's urging, his parents transferred him to a residential care facility in nearby El Monte that cares for forty other mentally ill patients, most of them schizophrenic. His condition continued to deteriorate over the years to the point where he feels comfortable living among people whose pace and ambition is similar to his. He still believes his bones are dissolving; schizophrenics often have delusions that are firmly held beliefs. He still studies the night sky and his mental alertness has recently improved with one of the new drugs.

Dr. Day—remains optimistic that current research will discover a treatment to make Bill well enough to function in society, and is encouraged by Bill's response to new drugs. Because of the way Bill's illness has progressed, Dr. Day feels that he will probably never be the astronomer he had dreamed of becoming. Nevertheless, as he always tells other families trying to cope with schizophrenia, he never gives up hope that someone—soon—will discover a cure for this devastating disorder and his patients can become the people they were meant to be when they were very young.

Clarke McAllister—remains heartbroken about Bill's mental illness, but no longer blames bizarre behavior or confused thinking on "my son's extraordinary imagination." He and Libby joined San

Gabriel Valley NAMI in Pasadena, a chapter of the California Alliance for the Mentally Ill, and have been comforted by the support and experience of its members. He is researching the extent to which various health insurance policies cover mental illness, and plans to present his findings at a statewide seminar planned for next spring.

Libby McAllister—has completed the first draft of her young adult novel about a sixteen-year-old girl whose eighteen-year-old brother becomes schizophrenic and is optimistic that she will find a publisher. *The Star News* published an op-ed she wrote about a mother trying to cope with her son's mental illness. El Monte is a short drive from Pasadena so she goes down to the Mesa Hills Guest Home often. Bill comes home for visits often, and enjoys being with the family, although he does little more than sit in the kitchen with Trixie. His old room is the way he left it, but after a few hours, he seems anxious to go back to his companions at the board and care home.

Ian Quinn—was awarded third prize in a prestigious *Los Angeles Times* photography contest. The picture was of students in the village of Sierra Madre suspended from ceiling ropes as they pasted flowers on the float they planned to enter in the Pasadena Rose Parade on New Year's Day. Because of the professional quality of his portfolio, "California Characters," Ian was granted a partial scholarship to Claremont College in that nearby town. He plans to major in journalism and photography.

Eric Bergman—still is not sure what he wants to do now that he has graduated from Wilson High. The tennis pro at the Beverly Hills Country Club has offered him a job, promising to teach him all he knows. Eric may take him up on it. He thinks he may get good enough at tennis to some day give private lessons.

BVG

Joannie Fargo—will enter the Pasadena City College School of Cosmetology in the fall to study for the state boards and become a certified cosmetologist. She talks about becoming beauty salon manager in a large hotel or on a cruise ship and saving enough money to attend the International School of Cosmetology in London. Eventually she hopes to own her own salon and spa, perhaps in Malibu or Marina del Rey.

Sheila Montgomery—has been accepted at the University of Pennsylvania School of Veterinary Medicine where she plans to specialize in the care of large animals, either in zoos or in their natural habitat. She explains that with giraffes she can dress as comfortably as she wants although she no longer dresses as sloppily as a bag lady. When her sister, Barbara, turned thirteen she became difficult to handle, had to be put on stronger medication and transferred to a locked facility. The last time Sheila visited her, Barbara didn't seem to recognize her and slapped her face. Sheila and Dana have remained friends and promise to write to each other while they are away at school.

Dana McAllister—had a wonderful senior year at Wilson High. She joined the girls' track team and made a lot of new friends working on the yearbook. Helping her mother with the dialogue for the new book gave her an interest in writing, but she still isn't sure what she will major in when she attends University of California, Santa Barbara in the fall. For now, she has chosen child psychology as a major. She is anxious to start college and her bags are half-packed already. Ian will help her move her stuff up. It saddens her to visit Bill in the place where he lives in El Monte because their lives have become so different. He asked her to get material on the college astronomy courses for him to take a look at, and she promised she would.